D0881204

A WAGON TRAIN
FOR BRIDES

A WAGON TRAIN FOR BRIDES

•

Kent Conwell

AVALON BOOKS
NEW YORK

PRINTED IN THE UNITED STATES OF AMERICA
ON ACID-FREE PAPER
BY HADDON CRAFTSMEN, BLOOMSBURG, PENNSYLVANIA

To Kay Resnick, a lovely woman who offered a precious gift to every writer she knew. Her enthusiasm, her encouragement made us all believe we deserved the Nobel Prize. And right now in Writer's Heaven, she's imbuing Hemingway, Faulkner, Steinbeck, and the thousands of others with the same enthusiasm and encouragement. We miss her.

And to my wife, Gayle. I love you.

Chapter One

The first thought that popped into my head when I met the Colonel was that he didn't look like any colonel I had known. He looked just like any other working cowpoke in faded jeans, worn denim shirt, leather vest slick with wear, and a ten-gallon sombrero that had once been white. The only apparel new about him was his boots with shiny Mexican silver heel- and toe-caps.

The next thought that popped into my head after I heard his proposition was that someone had beaten him over the head with a branch from the crazy tree.

But when he nailed me with those icy blue eyes and a handshake that felt like I'd stuck my hand in a vise, I reckoned there was more substance to him than I first guessed. And when he started talking, I knew he was an hombre used to getting his way. The tone in

1

his voice left no question that he was dead certain of everything he said and would tolerate arguments from no one.

He eyed the six-guns on my hips and then nodded to the seat across the table as he plopped down in his own chair. He hooked his thumb at the young, red-haired jasper beside him who wore a constant grin on his freckled face. "This here is Lay. Lafayette Fontaine Baker, but we call him Lay." He poured three glasses of Old Crow whiskey, downed his in one gulp, then fixed his eyes on mine. "I got a job that needs doing, and I heard you're a no-nonsense head knocker who can get things done."

I paid no attention to his flattery. What he said was true, and I didn't figure the truth to be flattery. I was a money-in-the-bank ramrod. Jaspers hired me to get a job done, and I did it. No nonsense. Besides, I was just off a cattle drive and at loose ends. I sipped my whiskey and shrugged. "Shoot."

He shot.

When Colonel Wilt Egerton had finished explaining his job offer to me, I knew I had been wrong about someone taking after him with a branch from the crazy tree. No, sir. They'd gone after him with the whole tree.

All I could do was stammer.

His eyes glittered with a touch of amusement. He leaned forward, resting his elbows on the saloon table. His tanned face reminded me of old leather. "Well, Mister Forrest. What do you say?"

I glanced at Lay. He wore a broad grin on his face.

"Did I hear you right, Colonel? Did you say a wagon train full of brides-to-be? Women?"

He leaned back and nodded slowly. "Well, at least there ain't nothing wrong with your hearing. That's what I said. I got me a big spread and a heap of cow-pokes that are anxious to find themselves a decent woman and settle down. Those old boys was ready to leave me. So, I had me a choice. Find them boys some brides or find me new wranglers. And I reckoned brides were easier to find than dependable wranglers. They're mighty fine cowmen, I tell you."

He poured another drink and downed it. He drew the back of his hand across his mouth. "Well, I found twenty-eight good and decent ladies, and now I got to get them to Palo Pinto down close to the Texas hill country. My ramrod up and got hisself shot dead two nights ago in a poker game. That's why I came to you. So, what about it?" He fished a bag of Bull Durham from his vest pocket.

I hedged on giving him an answer. "How'd you come to find me?"

Pursing his lips, he rolled the cigarette. He lit it and squinted through the smoke at me. "I saw the cattle in the pens down by the river. Someone said they come up from Fort Worth and that you was the jasper what ramrodded them up here. I heard you lost less than fifty out of two thousand head and ran over a gang of would-be rustlers. I figure anyone who can push two thousand head of long-legged Mexican cattle five hundred miles can manage a train load of women."

The young man's grin grew wider.

I reached for the bottle of Old Crow and filled my glass again. I sipped it. "Well, now Colonel. I don't reckon I'd want to start comparing women and cattle. It's been my experience that on occasion a single woman can cause a heap more trouble than two thousand head of ornery beeves."

The Colonel's grin split his leathery face in two. "I'm willing to make it worth your while. Get them ladies to Palo Pinto and you can take your pick between three thousand dollars or twenty-five hundred and sixty acres. That's four square miles of choice riverfront. Either way, I'd call that good wages."

I was speechless, so I gulped my drink and rolled a cigarette to gather my thoughts. "I can't argue that." I nodded to his young friend. "What about Lay here?"

The young man spoke up. "I ain't no ramrod, Mister Forrest. Just a hand."

Colonel Egerton broke in, a half grin on his weathered face. "Lay. How about getting us a fresh bottle?"

The young man nodded. "Yes, sir."

As Lay headed for the bar, the Colonel leaned forward. He kept his voice low. "Lay come to me when he was a youngster, an orphan. He just showed up one day. He can't handle this job. He knows it. He needs more seasoning. The way he's going, he'll be a top hand in a few more years. Lay and me talked about it. He's like a colt that's got to be brought along. He understands. Right now, I need someone like you, a seasoned, trail-wise bronco that won't let nothing stand in his way."

I wasn't falling for his honeyed words. "What about

you, Colonel? You look fit enough to yank the kinks out of a green bronc."

The smile flickered momentarily, then flared once again. "It's the heart, Mister Forrest. Doc says I'm borrowing time from God above. I got to be sure them ladies get through."

"Four sections of land or three thousand greenbacks is a heap to pay for a ramrod, Colonel."

He chuckled. "Son, I got two hundred sections. I ain't going to miss four. And on top of that, once we hit the trail, you get paid. Even if we don't make it past the Kansas border."

My tongue twisted around my eyeteeth so tight, I couldn't even stutter out a response.

Chapter Two

Smoke hung heavy in the saloon like a morning fog over the prairie. Cowpokes stood shoulder to shoulder at the bar, laughing, cursing. Gamblers intent on their cards hunkered over the poker tables, their eyes darting from one player to another. A tinny piano banged out a rendition of *Buffalo Gal* and an ungraceful line of hurdy-gurdy gals stomped across the stage.

But the Colonel's offer had made me feel like I was in a world of my own. I wasn't interested in the land. It was the three thousand that got my attention. Along with the three hundred dollars for the cattle drive I'd just completed, I'd have stake enough for a spread of my own. I'd always admired the rolling hills north of Fort Worth. Maybe I could find me a place around there.

Lay returned with an unopened bottle of Old Crow.

At the Colonel's nod, he opened the bottle and poured drinks around once again.

"You already got wagons and animals, Colonel?"

"Yep." He nodded. "Best I could buy. Reckon I should say, best that was left. There's still a heap of folks pushing west on the Santa Fe and Oregon trails. I'm using oxen. Slower, but more likely to get us there."

He hesitated, waiting for my opinion, I guessed. "Ox, huh? Good conditions, you'll get two miles an hour from them. Lucky if you average ten miles a day. How far is Palo Pinto?"

Colonel Egerton built another cigarette. "Six hundred miles or so, I reckon. Maybe a little less."

"That's a good two months—three if we run into much trouble. Going to be mighty hot."

He didn't reply. He simply stared at me. "Well, Mister Forrest. What do you say?"

"When are you moving out?"

"Soon as I can. In the morning if you're my man."

One thing about Colonel Egerton, he was not the kind to wait around for the bark to pop off a rail before he did something. I considered the offer. Herding twenty-eight females shouldn't be any more of a headache than pushing two thousand wild Mexican steers. Besides, I'd have plenty of help. I extended my hand. "The name is John Howard Forrest, Colonel. Call me Howie."

A broad grin split his face. He pumped my hand. "Fine." He pushed to his feet. "Come on, Howie. I'll show you the wagons and animals."

I followed after him, not aware of what I had gotten myself into.

The small town of Westport hummed with activity. Any town that took over from Independence as the trailhead for the Santa Fe Trail was bound to be busier than a flock of crows in a freshly plowed field. Four miles north was Westport Landing, where the ships and barges unloaded trade goods from the east.

Earlier, the trailhead had been Independence a few miles northeast. Before Independence, settlers pushed off from Franklin, miles to the east. Who could tell? Perhaps in a few years the trailhead would move on out to Lawrence to the west.

I swung onto my dun pony outside the saloon and fell in beside Lay and the Colonel as their ponies trotted down the dusty street. On either side, men scurried along the boardwalks in every direction. Women in gaily-colored hoop skirts and puffy sleeves stood out like bright flowers among the drab apparel of the men. Wagons of every description lined the street, bulky ambulances, fragile surreys, sturdy buckboards, square-sided Mormon wagons, massive Murphy wagons with their seven-foot wheels, lumbering Conestogas, and broad-bed freight wagons.

Loud voices carried on the hot, still air. In the distance, I heard sporadic gunfire.

"Busy place," said the Colonel.

"Yep." I didn't like busy places.

"Yonder's the wagons," he said when we reached the outskirts of town.

I looked in the direction he was pointing. A few hundred yards distant was a weathered barn and corral. Seven emigrant wagons with white duck bonnets stood side by side near the corral, which was filled with oxen and few ponies. The eighth wagon was parked near a fire blazing in front of the corral.

"There's Elijah now."

An elderly black man limped around the fire on a twisted leg. "Your greasybelly?"

Lay answered. "Best cook you'll ever see, Howie. Old Elijah can take the toughest cut of meat and make you think it's the choice off the backstrap."

Cattle drives always carried a chuck wagon. I reckoned the Colonel had one for his own men. At that moment, a small boy crawled from under the chuck wagon and spoke to Elijah.

"Looks like your man's made a friend in town."

The Colonel grunted. "Nope. That's Nelly Jackson's boy."

"Nelly Jackson?" I hoped he wasn't going to say what I thought he was going to say.

He said it. "She's one of our ladies. The only one with an offspring. I started not to take her, but her husband rode with Mosby." He shook his head. "That was good enough for me."

I started to protest, but changed my mind. One boy couldn't hurt much. Besides, his mother would be along to look after him. Instead, I changed the subject. "How many riders you have?"

Lay glanced up at the Colonel, a worried look in his eyes.

Colonel Egerton reined up and surveyed the wagons. "All we need," he boomed. "Eight. A dozen altogether, counting the three of us," he replied, making a brief gesture with his hand. "And Elijah."

Suddenly, I was apprehensive. "You mean . . . What about drivers? Who's handling the teams?"

He looked at me as if I had three heads. "Why, the women, naturally."

Another round of gunshots echoed from behind the barn. The Colonel dipped his head in that direction. Just as casually as you would ask for a drink of water, he said. "That's them now. The boys are teaching them how to shoot. Been working with them for the last week. Reckon we'll need them when we hit Indian Territory."

I stared at him in disbelief as my suddenly numbed brain struggled to absorb his words. The young boy was one thing, but now—surely, he didn't mean what I thought he meant. I glanced at Lay, who wore a broad grin on his face. Turning back to the Colonel, I stammered. "You're . . . you're saying the women are going to drive the oxen and protect the wagons?"

He eyed me levelly. "I not only expect them to do it, Howie, but I expect them to do it as well as a man."

"But, they're women. They're supposed to be in the kitchen. That's their place. Women can't do things like a man. It ain't . . . What I mean is that ain't the way things are supposed to be. I figured they'd be riding in the wagons. This way, they're going to be walking six hundred miles. They won't make it. They're too puny."

Another round of gunfire echoed from behind the barn.

Colonel Egerton leaned back in his saddle. "You know, Howie. When I was a younker, I knew an old boy so narrow-minded that he could see through a keyhole with both eyes. A jasper like that can't see none of the miracles that can come about in this world. I'm banking a heap that them women not only can drive oxen and shoot, but if the need arises, they'll learn to fork a horse as good as a man. Besides," he added, "I got a hole card."

I eyed him dubiously, wondering if I could find some way to gracefully crawfish out of our deal. "It must be a high one."

He grinned. His leathery face crinkled into lines deeper than a canyon. "It'll beat an ace any day. I'm giving them ladies a new life. The chance to go to a new country and start all over. They want it bad. That's why I figure they'll make it."

I studied the older man. I figured this whole gamble was going to crumble around his shoulders. Women were women. They'd break down and bawl as soon as their hair got mussed. But despite my sudden reservations about his wild scheme, I liked Colonel Wilt Egerton. I shrugged. I didn't mind giving anyone a chance, even the ladies. And since I didn't have anything better to do, and since he was willing to pay me more than I could make in a year of pushing beeves, I'd play my cards to the end.

"That being the case, Colonel, you done right getting the oxen. Even a child can walk alongside a team of oxen and handle them with a Moses' Stick."

He winked at Lay. The young man chuckled. "That's why the Colonel got them, Howie. Except for Elijah. That old man wouldn't have come if he couldn't have his mules."

Colonel Egerton chuckled. "He's so crippled up, he couldn't make half a day on foot."

As we headed for the barn, the Colonel continued. "I put four women to each wagon. They take turns driving the team. The others can walk or ride."

"Walk? What about horses? They're riding, aren't they?"

He eyed me a moment, a brief grin ticking up one side of his lips. "Nope. Think about it. Twenty-one more horses, twenty-one more saddles? I'm not concerned about the cost, but figure the extra work with that many animals. Besides, they can only go as fast as the oxen. Just that much less trouble you boys will have each morning and night."

I saw his point.

We reined up at the corner of the barn and looked on as the women continued their target practice. Their targets were odd items, cans, boxes, stumps, rocks.

To my surprise, some of the ladies were downright proficient with the rifles. I looked closer. They were using Winchesters. "Mighty powerful weapon for some of those smaller ladies, Colonel."

He studied them carefully. "Reckon so, Howie. Most of them are wearing some powerful-looking bruises, but they stuck to it. That's what I meant earlier. They got one last chance to have the kind of life they dream of. I don't think they'll let me down."

I sat on my pony for a few minutes watching the ladies who were all shapes and sizes. Some wore men's pants, some long skirts. All wore some kind of bonnet against the sun.

The Colonel said, "I bought them all Winchester 1866s."

"A good rifle," I replied, patting my own in the boot. The 1866 with the .44 rimfire and 28 grains of powder was a sound rifle—a bit underpowered for big game other than deer, but with its fifteen-cartridge tubular magazine, twenty-eight women could put on quite a show for a band of marauding Comancheros or Kiowas.

A few of the ladies flinched when they fired the Winchester, but most, even the tiny ones, clenched their teeth and stood up to the kick of the relatively new repeater.

The Colonel pointed out a tiny woman who probably didn't weigh ninety pounds soaking wet. She stood straight and firm when she fired, and her slugs hit her target every time. "That's Nelly Jackson, the boy's Ma. His name's Homer."

I had to admit, I was getting my eyes full, but I didn't figure we had no more chance of making Palo Pinto than a grasshopper with two broken legs in the middle of a flock of starving roosters.

After a spell, we rode back to the fire where we squatted with a cup of coffee. It was thick and black, what I always called six-shooter coffee because you could float a six-shooter on it.

Elijah was an ex-slave from Louisiana. He'd been greasybellying for the Colonel for over forty years. I'm usually pretty much of a loner. I don't have what a jasper could call a sidekick or best friend. I reckon if I died, they'd have to rent mourners.

Like I said I usually don't take to people, but Elijah was a bright-eyed and genial old man whom I liked immediately, just as I liked Lay and the Colonel. And that was unusual for me.

I figured out the reason sometime later, but at the time, I was too thick-headed to see what was plain before my eyes.

A heavy pot of beans and meat bubbled over the fire. Two large coffeepots sat in the coals. Elijah limped to the chuck wagon. "Vittles ready when you is, Colonel. Steak and beans. Biscuits in the spider."

The Colonel looked at me. "Howie?"

I held up my coffee. "This'll do for now. I put myself around a steak just before we had our talk."

"Suit yourself," he replied, rising and filling a tin plate and refreshing his coffee. Lay tagged along. They both squatted beside me and started shoveling grub down their gullets.

The Colonel explained how he planned on four women in each wagon with their belongings and grub. "They'll take turns driving and riding shotgun. Elijah will carry the wrangler's soogans in the chuck wagon."

"How much grub you get for them?"

He shook his head. "A heap. Two hundred pounds of flour, thirty of hardtack for each wagon. Then bacon, rice, coffee, sugar, dried beans, salt, baking soda, dried fruit, cornmeal and parched corn."

I arched an eyebrow. The Colonel knew what he was about.

Lay took a mouthful of a biscuit, smacked his lips, and winked at me. "Oughta try some of Elijah's biscuits, Mist . . . I mean, Howie."

About that time, three of the Colonel cowpokes stomped up to the fire. With sullen grimaces on their faces, they nodded to the Colonel and Lay, frowned at me, then heaped their plates with grub.

"Might as well," I said to Lay. I called out. "Be much obliged if you'd toss me one of those biscuits, Elijah."

The old man hesitated for a moment, deferring to one of the wranglers. When the cowpoke stepped back from the spider, Elijah reached for a biscuit.

One of the Colonel's wranglers, a heavy-bearded, thick-jawed jasper, growled and shoved Elijah away from the spiderful of biscuits. "You don't touch none of that grub meant for a white man, Boy!"

I never had trouble reacting to problems in my life. That's probably why I never made many friends. If that was the price, I didn't mind.

Elijah had not stumbled back three steps before I spun the lantern-jawed cowpoke around and slammed my fist into the bridge of his nose, smashing it over his face and splattering his blood on his compadres standing nearby.

He yowled in pain, dropped his plate, and staggered backwards over the fire, sprawling to the ground. He bounced up like a rubber ball, his hands pressed over his nose, and his eyes wild with fury. Blood ran from between his fingers and dripped from his chin.

Everyone else just stood stock-still, mouths open, stunned by the suddenness of my attack.

Blood poured through his fingers, dripped off his chin onto his chest. He glared at me. "Why, you no—"

I hit him again, first with an overhand right, then a left hook into his ribs. He screamed in pain and doubled over. That's when I straightened him with a right uppercut to the point of his chin.

He hit the ground unconscious.

Taking a step back, I lowered my hands and turned to the awed faces staring at me. I looked each of the astonished cowpokes in the eye. "The Colonel here hired me to push this wagon train to the Texas hill country. I agreed. That means I'm running the whole shebang." I nodded to the unconscious man. "He's out of here. I don't tolerate one body mistreating another. I don't care if they're red, brown, black, yellow, or blue. I've got friends among them all. And while I'm saying my piece, there won't be no whiskey, no gambling, or no consorting with the ladies on this drive. If you boys can't live with those rules, then you best light a shuck out of here."

Several moments of silence followed.

Then a feminine voice sang out. "What about us, Mister Boss Man? Same rules?"

I jerked around, searching for the speaker. A young

woman in her early twenties with dark hair stepped forward. She wore men's jeans and a red plaid shirt was tucked in about the waist. She glared at me, her hands on her hips, and a gleam in her eyes that seemed to dare me to argue with her.

Several ladies stood behind her, all eyeing me curiously. My ears burned, but I matched her stare.

From the corner of my eye, I could see Colonel Egerton looking back and forth between the two of us. I hadn't really planned on talking to the ladies, but now the question had been asked. I replied. "Yes, Ma'am. Same rules. No whiskey, no gambling, and no consorting with the hired men."

She arched an amused eyebrow. "Oh, good. We were afraid you might have rules against knitting or combing our hair."

The ladies behind her snickered. I heard Colonel Egerton cough nervously.

I'm not real swift at times, but a jasper didn't need to be swift to recognize the sarcasm in her words. I shook my head. "No, Ma'am. I reckon as long as you ladies are content with knitting and primping, I'll be satisfied. But," I added emphatically. "If you let your knitting or primping get in the way of the job I'm being paid to do, then I'll make more rules. And if that don't work, I might have to spank somebody."

The smiles faded from their faces. They set their jaws and as one, glared at me.

I continued, figuring that maybe I had pushed them a tad too far with my last remark. Still, her snide comments stuck in my craw. "Now the Colonel here says he expects each of you to handle a team of oxen and take care of yourself with the Winchester. If there are any of you who expect some man to take care of you, you're in the wrong place. You'd best pack up and go back to town now. On this trip, you're expected to take care of yourself and each other."

The dark-haired woman stepped forward. "None of us would be here, Mister Trail Boss, if we wanted help from you men." Her dark eyes stared at me. "Colonel Egerton has given us the chance to start over. We can take care of ourselves. Don't you worry."

I've always been uncomfortable around women, and I was downright uncomfortable now. But, I had meant what I said. "Well, Miss . . ." I hesitated.

She tilted her chin. "Katherine Louise Stanton." Her icy reply would have frozen a tub of ice cream in two minutes.

"Well, Miss Stanton. I'm pleased to hear that. But the Colonel here pays me to worry, and until I get you ladies to Palo Pinto, I'll continue to worry."

She eyed me another few seconds, and then with a toss of her head, strode past the fire to her wagon. The other ladies followed.

Two of the unconscious cowpoke's compadres helped him to his feet and led him into the barn. Moments later, the three rode out.

Chapter Three

Colonel Egerton chuckled. "Well, Howie. For your first time meeting them ladies, I reckon you did fine. You held your own, more or less until you got to the spanking part. 'Course, we lost three of our wranglers."

There was no reproof in his eyes, just the calm acceptance of what had been done. I glanced at the five cowpokes remaining. They were sitting around the fire cross-legged downing their chow. None appeared upset that I had run three of them off.

I replied to the Colonel in a voice loud enough for them to hear. "Those kind of jaspers, we can find anywhere. I learned long ago that it don't take any more time or any skin off a jasper's nose to treat other folks decent. In fact, it generally makes life easier for everyone concerned. As far as our ladies, I don't know what

19

I expected, but at least I got through my first meeting with them without any gunplay."

We all chuckled. I continued, "Reckon you're right about them. I suppose things did go as fine as a frog hair split down the middle." I didn't feel as confident as I sounded.

That night around the fire, I laid out my route for the Colonel. The five wranglers eased forward to see my plan. Using a branch, I punched a hole in the sand. "Here we are, Westport. Down here is Fort Gibson." I punched another hole and drew a line in the sand joining the two. "We head due south to Fort Gibson. From there we hit the Texas Road to the Red River. From the Red, we'll take the Marcy Trail past Jacksboro and Fort Griffin. There we'll cut south again."

He studied the lines I had drawn in the sand. He took the branch from me and laid out his route due west. "I figured the Santa Fe Trail over to Fort Dodge and then turn south."

I rolled a cigarette. "Do that and you'll be crossing the Staked Plains in the middle of drought season. My way, the only dry spot is a stretch just this side of Jacksboro. Besides, your way is longer."

A gust of wind stirred the fire. Sparks skittered across the sandy ground. Lay sat beside us, watching silently.

"You familiar with the route?" The Colonel eyed me closely.

"I brought the herd up the trail from the Red. It's been a couple years since I been on the Marcy Trail, but we ain't had no particular dry spell down there so I reckon we won't have water problems. Just past Jacksboro is the Brazos River. From there on, you got more water than you know what to do with."

Murmurs came from the onlooking cowpokes. One of them spoke up. "I come from there a few weeks back. There's a couple small streams between the Red and Jacksboro, Boss. No problem there."

I nodded to him.

One of the others spoke up. "What about Kiowa or Comanche?"

"Might run into a few. The Comanche are staying up in the Panhandle. Around Palo Duro Canyon. I reckon what few we run into we'll be able to handle with the firepower we have."

The Colonel studied the lines in the sand. He cleared his throat. "Well, Howie. I'm paying you top wages to guide us. I reckon I ain't so foolish as to dispute what you're telling me. Otherwise, I'd save my money and do what I wanted to do."

Elijah poured us a cup of coffee. I sipped mine. It was hot and thick. "Trust me, Colonel. It's the best way."

He and Lay exchanged looks. Then he nodded. "We'll go your way, Howie."

The cowpoke who had first spoken came up to me. He extended his hand. "I'm Joe Allen, Boss." He hooked his thumb to a grinning, tow-headed boy not over seventeen. "This here's my kid brother, Emmett. You won't have no trouble from us."

I shook his hand. "Thanks, Joe. Emmett."

The other three stepped forward. The youngest of the three was Cole Haywood. His sun-bleached hair hung down about his shoulders and a happy-go-lucky gleam glittered in his eyes. The other two were older, in their forties, I guessed. Longtime drifters. Pot-bellied Ed Dowling was missing four teeth in the middle, and the others were black with rot. Tobacco juice dribbled from either side of his lips down onto his grizzled chin. Albert Thigpen was twig-thin, and he loved to whistle.

"Well, boys, you give the Colonel an honest day's work, we got no problems. Just stay away from the women, the cards, and the booze." I dropped my empty cup in the tub of boiling water. "Since you're wanting to move out in the morning, Colonel, reckon I'll ride in and pick up my plunder from the hotel."

Westport was typical of trailhead cities. Saloons ran twenty-four hours; whiskey sold for a nickel a shot; crib girls called from balconies; card sharks stole from the greenhorns; storeowners sold goods to anxious emigrants at two hundred percent profit; and hundreds of pioneers sprawled in their wagons each night too excited to sleep.

The streets buzzed with traffic. The only difference in noon and midnight was the sun in the sky. I made my way down the busy street to the Westport Hotel where I had tossed my soogan with the other wranglers' gear in one corner of the lobby. To my surprise, none of our plunder was where we had left it.

The bell clerk hastily explained that hotel management had demanded the gear be removed, so a couple of our boys had hauled it all over to the livery stable. I headed for the livery.

Sure enough, it was all heaped in one stall. I dug mine out. While I was tying it behind the cantle of my saddle, the livery doors swung open and the three jaspers I'd run off staggered in, sixguns in hand. They were drunk.

"Figured we'd find you here," growled the lantern-jawed one I had coldcocked earlier.

"Yeah." Another one chimed in. "And keep your hands where we can see them."

My pony perked his ears. He stutter-stepped nervously. I kept my hands on the soogan in plain sight. I studied them from across the rump of my dun. "You got me at a disadvantage, boys. Is that how you always play the game?"

They stiffened at the sarcasm in my words. "Step out from behind that horse, Boss Man." The flickering light from the barn lantern cast a yellow pall on their faces. They were drunk enough to kill. And I was the one they wanted.

"Okay, boys. Just let me get away from my pony. I don't want him hurt when I lay you out for a pine box."

My gall shocked them. One of the three hesitated. He cast a nervous glance at the others. I took a step to one side, my hands to my side. "Gun me down without a chance, and the law will have you for murder." I took another step to my right.

Lantern Jaw guffawed. "So you say, but there ain't going to be nobody around to say what happened. Besides, my cousin is sheriff hereabouts. He won't care what nobody says except me." His dark eyes glittered.

The other two chuckled.

I tensed my muscles, ready to make my move. "Oh, no? What about that jasper over in the corner?" I dipped my head to the right.

"Huh?" The three glanced in the corner. That was all I needed. I dropped into a crouch, shucking my Navy Colt at the same time. Three deafening explosions that ran together as one deafened my ears and thick, acrid smoke filled the livery. The three bushwhackers screamed and stumbled back, sprawling on the ground. Horses whinnied and kicked their stalls.

Quickly, I holstered my six-gun and led my pony out the back door of the barn into the corral. In the distance, I heard voices and running feet heading for the livery. The last thing I needed was to get stuck in town for a coroner's inquiry.

Remaining calm, I led my dun from the corral and then slowly around in front of the livery where a crowd was quickly gathering. Nonchalantly, I nudged one of the onlookers. "What happened?"

He looked around and shook his head. "Don't know. Some kind of shooting."

I clucked my tongue and shook my head. "Too bad. Seemed like a peaceful town, too." I climbed into the saddle. I looked over the heads of the crowd and saw several hombres gathered around the three bushwhackers lying on the ground. I squeezed the dun's ribs. "Let's go, boy."

* * *

Back at the camp, I informed Colonel Egerton of the incident. He stared at the mug of steaming coffee he cupped gingerly in his hands and shook his head. "Don't let it bother you, Howie."

"It don't. I just don't cotton to causing you any problems, Colonel. I got a mind for me to ride out. Families stick together, and what with his cousin the sheriff, I don't figure we've heard the end of this."

The expression on his weathered face didn't change. "You stay. Like you say, them boys pushed it. I learned young that a jasper shouldn't put no more on his plate than he can eat. The sheriff decides to push it, then we'll see just how much he heaps on his plate."

I refilled my cup and leaned back against the wagon wheel. "Thanks, Colonel."

Chapter Four

I slept little that night. Each time I heard pounding hooves, I stopped worrying about the problems the women would cause and started looking for the sheriff and his deputies. I hoped I hadn't killed anyone in the livery, but I had to shoot fast, too fast to place any shots.

But as each set of hoofbeats faded, my worries about the upcoming journey came flooding back. Doubts filled my head. I couldn't imagine twenty-eight frail, pouting women walking six hundred miles guiding a team of six oxen. I figured that the first thunderstorm would probably end the expedition. If not, then the second one.

I rolled over in my soogan and pulled the blanket up around my neck. What the Sam Hill. Either way, I got paid.

Finally, well before sunup, Elijah stoked up the banked fire, put on coffee, dropped sourdough in the spider, and flopped strips of steak in the skillet.

I glanced toward Westport. Still no sheriff. I was ready to light a shuck out of town before he showed up.

Lanterns came on in the wagons, and soon our party was bustling about, rigging up the animals, stowing gear, and making ready for the big moment.

The grub simmered in heavy pots. Elijah grabbed the dipper from a pot of bubbling redeye gravy and banged it around the triangle. He cried out, "Come and get it. I'm throwing it out in five minutes." He dropped the dipper back in the gravy and set about harnessing up his animals.

The ladies clustered about, chattering, laughing, downing coffee, and wrapping fried steak in oilcloth for the noon meal. They acted like youngsters anticipating their first box supper and dance.

I gathered the wranglers around the fire. "Move among them, boys. Make sure everything's hooked up right. And whatever you do, stay out of in front of their Winchesters."

The boys chuckled, but a strident woman's voice cut off their laughter. "I suppose you think that's funny, Mister Forrest."

I looked around and groaned. Katherine Stanton. Of all who might have overheard me, it had to be Katherine Stanton. "No, Ma'am," I managed to reply. "Just an observation, but I truly believe a sensible one."

She glared at us, then spun on her heel and stormed back to her wagon.

I watched as the ladies rigged the yokes on the oxen. Each wagon had three yokes, two oxen each yoke for a total of six oxen for each wagon. I couldn't help admiring the Colonel's foresight. Two yoke of oxen could probably have made the journey without trouble, but the third yoke was sound insurance.

More and more, I was coming to believe the Colonel meant business.

As the women busied themselves, I checked each wagon, testing the fit of the bows around the neck of the oxen, yanking on the wheels to make sure the nuts were tight on the axle, and any of a hundred other small items that could go wrong once we hit the trail.

Pausing at one wagon, I watched the four ladies working together. I don't know exactly what I expected, but I got me a surprise. A large-boned woman wearing men's clothing and standing a couple inches taller than me barked the orders. The ladies yoked the first two oxen and then the large-boned woman backed the team up to the wagon where a lady on either side chained the yoke to the bolster. That team was the wheelers. By now, the fourth woman had backed the middle or swing team in front of the wheelers and the ladies chained the yoke to the wheelers' yoke. The large woman then backed the lead team in. While she inserted the wagon tongue through the ring in the yoke, the others chained the lead team to the swing yoke.

"Good job, ladies," I said.

The large-boned woman eyed me skeptically. "You just do your job as well, Boss Man." Her eyes glittered with defiance.

I couldn't resist grinning at her grit. "Name's Howie, ma'am. And I'll hold up my end. Just see you ladies do."

"I'm Bertha Lewis. I answer to Bertha. And you don't worry none about us, Mister Howie. We'll get it done."

I glanced at Lay who sat astride his sorrel beside me. He arched an eyebrow in approval. I nodded. "If they're all like her, I reckon I don't need to worry none." Of course, I knew they weren't. So I continued to worry. I glanced toward town anxiously.

Near the end of the train, I spotted Katherine Stanton. She wore a blue gingham dress, a sunbonnet, and brogans. I nodded as I rode past. She ignored me.

I had assigned our outriders their spots. Emmett and Cole were the youngest, so I put them in drag with the remuda of oxen. Joe Allen would ride point, and the two old wranglers, Thigpen and Dowling, I put out as swingers. Elijah would lead out. The rest of us would do what needed to be done when it had to be done.

Colonel Egerton reined up. "Well, Howie?"

I glanced to the east. False dawn was graying the horizon. "Looks like we're about ready, Colonel."

Our route lay smack down the main street of Westport, right in front of the sheriff's office. I walked my dun along the wagon train. The ladies looked up at me hopefully from their respective wagons. I could see the excitement in their eyes. One in each group held the Moses' Stick, a shoulder-length staff used to guide, encourage, or punish an ox.

I reined up beside Elijah in the lead wagon. "Ready?"

He nodded, his smile a sharp contrast to his dark skin. "Yes, sir."

I scooted around in my saddle. "Okay, ladies. Let's go to Texas."

We headed out, straight down the middle of Westport, eight wagons, seven women carrying a Moses' Stick walking beside the off wheeler, twenty-one women either perched in the wagons or striding alongside the wagons, and eight wranglers on horseback.

Folks stopped on the boardwalk and stared.

I kept my eyes on the sheriff's office.

As we passed, I spotted him standing at the window, idly watching. He raised a hand in a brief greeting. I touched my finger to the brim of my hat.

The Colonel had mentioned that Westport had been laid out on the Kansas–Missouri border. I reckoned that once west of town, we were in Kansas, and Missouri law couldn't touch me. I peered down the street, halfway expecting that invisible line to stand up and wave. Naturally, it did no such thing.

I hoped the Colonel was right.

As the brilliant orange globe of the sun rose over the black line of the horizon, we moved past the outskirts of town. I eased into the lead, heading due west for a few miles before cutting south. All around us, the ground was packed hard and bare of grass, a result of the westward migration over the last forty-odd years.

For the first few miles out of Westport, the Santa Fe Trail and the Oregon Trail were one. Then they separated, the Oregon heading for Lawrence and the Santa Fe for Council Grove.

I planned cutting south well before the split in the trail. My route would provide easy travel, for most of it ran through valleys and across rolling plains thick with lush bluestem grass. Although we would move through the foothills of the western Ozarks, I didn't figure on any treacherous mountains until we hit the Ouachitas.

An hour later, a shout caught my attention. I grimaced. A band of riders was approaching from Westport. I glanced over my shoulder, considering making a run.

The Colonel waved to me. I pulled up beside Elijah. "Keep 'em heading due west."

With a nod, he popped the reins against his mules' rumps and shouted at the animals. "Pick it up, Gabriel. Stay with him, Gideon. Gee, Moses. Move out, Abraham."

The ladies craned their necks as I rode past, curious.

The Colonel sat slumped in his saddle, eyeing the approaching riders. I noticed he'd flipped the loop off the hammer of his Colt.

I reined up.

"I reckon that's the sheriff," he muttered.

"I reckon."

Lay pulled up on the other side of the Colonel.

Half-a-dozen rugged looking hombres rode behind the sheriff. Two to one, but the numbers didn't bother me. With the first shot, horses would bolt, all except Blue, my dun. He was seven years old, and stood like a rock even when there was gunfire all around him. I'd ridden Blue through the Civil War when I rode with my cousin, Nathan Bedford Forrest. At Brice's Crossroads on June 10, 1864, my pony saw more fighting than a dozen average soldiers.

The Colonel nodded as the sheriff reined up. "What can I do for you, Sheriff?"

His men lined up on either side of him and glared at me. Lantern-jawed just like his cousin, he eyed me. "I got three jaspers back in town all shot up. They say you done it. One of them is my cousin."

My palm rested on top of my thigh. "Reckon they're right, Sheriff." I started to explain, then decided against it. I got me a stubborn streak that flares up at times, and this was one of them.

He tilted his head toward town. "Lucky for you, you didn't kill none of them. My cousin told me what happened. He was all likkered up. He's ornery, but honest for the most part." He hesitated, then turned back to the Colonel. "That ain't the reason I come out here." He rested his hands on the saddlehorn and leaned forward. "You got a woman on this here train by the name of Maude Perkins? Short." He paused and grimaced uncomfortably. "Kinda, well, round and all." His last words faded away.

I remembered seeing a woman that fit his description. I spoke up. "Why do you want to know, Sheriff?"

He glanced at me in surprise. He'd expected a reply from the Colonel.

I continued. "I'm the ramrod. I make the decisions on this drive. You want something, you talk to me."

Momentarily perplexed, he looked at the Colonel who replied with a trace of amusement in his tone. "You heard the man, Sheriff. He's the boss until we reach Palo Pinto."

My pony pranced nervously. I clicked my tongue and he steadied down. "Now, Sheriff. Once again. Why do you want her?"

He looked from the Colonel to me, then spit out the words. "Desertion and theft."

"Desertion?" I stifled a laugh. "Who'd she desert?"

He glanced around at his men. "Well, her husband, for one. She run off and left him. Took his horse too."

I chuckled. "Well, maybe he deserved it. That ever cross your mind? Besides, the horse belonged to her too if they were married."

The sheriff eyed me nervously.

Colonel Egerton interrupted. "Her husband, you say. So she is married?"

A hopeful look replaced the nervousness on the sheriff's face. "That's right. Married."

The Colonel sighed. "If she is married, Howie, then she lied. All these ladies are unmarried. I don't want none of my boys back in Palo Pinto to get hurt because of someone's lies."

I understood his point.

The sheriff gave me a smug sneer. He backed his pony. "I'll go get her now," he said.

I spurred my pony in front of the sheriff. "Not yet, Sheriff. You just wait here. I'll get her."

"You heard him," said the Colonel. "Lay and me here will just keep you old boys company until Howie comes back with Miz Perkins."

I waved Thigpen in as I made my way to Maude Perkins' wagon. She was round as a ball with a wide smile and laughing eyes. She wore her gray-streaked hair pulled back in a knot at the back of her head. A round-brimmed, straw hat with a clutch of faded cloth flowers on the crown perched crookedly on her head.

The laughter faded from her eyes when I explained what was taking place. She snorted. "Desertion? Why that long-legged, slack-jawed, worthless . . ." And then she described him in as colorful a language I had ever heard. She paused. "Just wait," she said, quickly disappearing through the puckered opening in the rear of the wagon. Moments later, she reappeared, stuffing a slip of paper in the pocket of the vest she wore over her faded gingham dress.

A rail-thin young woman in a worn shift and old brogans laid her arm on Maude's. "Let me go with you. You might need some help."

The roly-poly little woman smiled warmly and patted the younger woman's hand. "Don't worry, Matilda. I'll be fine. The Lord's with me."

I nodded to Thigpen. "Give her your pony. You can ride in the wagon until we get back."

To my surprise, despite her rotund body, Maude swung into the saddle like she'd been born to it. She jammed her heels into the pony's flanks and raced toward the waiting men. I had to hurry to keep up with her.

She yanked her mount to a sliding halt and glared at the sheriff. "Now, what's all this nonsense about?" She held the reins taut. Her strident demand caused the sheriff and his men to back up a step.

I had the feeling they saw their own Ma reincarnated in her solid little frame.

Colonel Egerton spoke up. "Seems like your husband filed charges on you for desertion and theft, Mrs. Perkins."

She shook her head. "That sounds like that no-account, Wylie. Here." She fished the slip of paper from her vest and shoved it into the Colonel's hands. "He ran off five years ago when our baby was sick. The little thing died because I didn't have no food and no doctor would come out unless he got paid. Them papers are the divorce papers. I divorced him two years ago."

The sheriff squirmed uncomfortably. "There's still the horse charge, Ma'am."

"He's a liar. He left me with nothing except a broken-down plow horse that died that winter. He even took what little money we had left. That wasn't the first time, but by jiminy, it was the last. He ran off, and my baby died because of that." She stared squarely into the sheriff's eyes. "That's the truth, Sheriff."

For several seconds, no one said a word. Then the sheriff cleared his throat and glanced around nervously. "Well, I believe you, Ma'am, but you best come back to Westport with me to straighten all this out."

Maude glanced up at me, her fearful eyes pleading for help.

Colonel Egerton spoke up. "No, Sheriff. I don't reckon she will. First, the little lady is legally divorced from her ex-husband." He held up the divorce decree, then handed it back to Maude. "Second, I believe her about the horse, and third, you're in Kansas now. You got no jurisdiction."

A crooked leer broke through the sheriff's heavy beard. He patted his six-gun. "This says I do."

Two of his men guffawed.

I spoke softly. "Pull that hogleg, Sheriff, and they'll be planting you under six feet of Missouri mud—or Kansas dirt, whichever you want."

The sheriff froze.

His voice calm and soft, the Colonel said, "Hold on, Howie. No need for that. Sheriff, I might look it to you, but I'm no drifting chuckline runner. I studied Missouri and Kansas laws before making this trip. Before I go anywhere, I learn the laws of that state. In section 432, paragraph six of the Missouri Penal Code, it states that any law enforcement officer pursing and apprehending a fugitive in another state will be subject to a five thousand–dollar fine, five years or both. And if you think I won't report you, Sheriff, you're mistaken."

The sheriff's eyes grew wide. He hesitated. He glanced at his men for support, but they simply shrugged and stared at the ground. He tried to bluff. "Who'd believe you. It's your word against mine and my boys here. Six to three."

The Colonel laughed. "You can't even count, Sheriff. It isn't six to three." He gestured over his shoulder. "It's thirty-seven to six. And what judge is going to call twenty-eight innocent and pure women liars?"

Fire blazed from the sheriff's eyes. The veins in his neck bulged.

I eased my hand back toward the butt of my six-gun.

The air vibrated with tension.

Finally, he backed away. He glared at me. "Just stay out of Westport, Mister. We don't need your kind."

I gave him a crooked grin. I guess he needed that final touch of bravado for his own ego. I didn't mind obliging him. "Don't worry. Staying out of your town will be the easiest thing I've every done, Sheriff."

We backed away a few steps, then turned and rode slowly back to the train. "Don't look back," the Colonel whispered. "We got nothing to worry about."

As we drew closer to the wagon train, I wondered about that law business. "Did you really do what you said, Colonel? I mean about looking up all those laws before you go someplace?"

Lay snickered.

The Colonel winked at me. "If I did, I'd be too busy to ever go anywhere."

"But, those figures you tossed out back there. Section, paragraph, all that foofaraw?"

"A little secret, Howie. There isn't a jasper alive who isn't impressed when you throw out important-sounding numbers. They just accept them. Never occurs to them you just made 'em up."

Maude laughed. "You're some gent, Colonel. You married?"

We joined in her laughter, but right then I recognized another one of the many reasons Colonel Egerton owned two hundred square miles of Texas.

I promised myself then I'd never play poker with him.

Chapter Five

The rolling prairies of Kansas reminded me of those back in Texas. Luxuriant bluestem and buffalo grass covered the gently undulating hills like a green quilt patched with brilliant splashes of yellow sunflowers, pink morning glories, and blue asters.

We continued west. I planned on staying west of the route I'd taken on the cattle drive, for graze was fairly thin where the great herds had traveled. Two thousand head of beeves don't leave much grass behind.

The euphoria of setting out on a great adventure faded for most of the ladies as the noonday sun baked the ground. Several who had started out walking beside their wagons had climbed back in. We stopped at noon for a short break and the second switch in bullwhackers.

The Colonel had figured that each team of four ladies could handle twelve hours a day bullwhacking. We'd make another switch in mid-afternoon, and end up just before dusk.

I rode up and down the train several times. There were a few small problems, but we quickly worked them out.

A couple hours before dusk, we turned south. I heard a heap of complaining. I was looking forward to our first night, wondering how many of our ladies would be wanting to turn back the next morning.

The morning after the first night on the trail was always difficult. Muscles would be stiff from the unaccustomed walking. Arms would ache after wielding the Moses' Stick. But if they wanted to reach their goal, they had to ignore the aches and pains and set about yoking their animals and building their breakfast, and all before the sun eased over the horizon.

I halfway grinned to myself. Yep. Tomorrow morning, we'd be taking a heap of them back to Westport.

Throughout the day, I couldn't help noticing Katherine Stanton and Bertha Lewis. The truth was, they didn't strike me as the kind who would back away, but then, the hard part of the journey had yet to begin.

Nelly Jackson, Homer's mother, did her part, and to my surprise and relief, the boy never got in the way. At least, not enough to cause problems.

Excited chatter drifted around our camp that first night. It always does the first night out, but as the long, long days pass, enthusiasm wanes, and soon the jour-

ney is a horrible, grueling ordeal of unbearable sun and choking dust and days that seem to never end.

The ladies sat around their fires, making plans, dreaming, wishing. I knew what it was like to want something, and then watch it slip away. Despite my firm conviction the ladies couldn't stand up to the rigors of the trip, I found myself hoping they would.

In the distance, a coyote wailed. A couple of the women gave a startled gasp. I called out, "Just coyotes, ladies. You might hear some skulking about. They'll usually run, but don't count on it. If you got to leave your wagons at night, take a lantern. Rattlesnakes like to hunt when it's cool. You spot one, don't stop to kill it. Get away. It'll go its own way."

My little warnings quieted some of the talk. Several of the ladies kept looking around at the darkness surrounding them. Those were the ones I figured we'd be taking back.

One, Virginia Lea Miller, a handsome woman with long blond hair, had begun complaining only hours out of Westport, and her complaints lasted all day. I didn't figure she would make it.

Emmett and Joe Allen took the first watch. Counting the extra ten head of oxen we had, fifty-two head of the lumbering beeves, a dozen ponies, and four mules were a heap easier to keep an eye on than two thousand ornery Mexican steers. Maybe we'd have good luck on this trip.

Unfortunately, we didn't. In fact, the bad luck began next morning.

*   *   *

The Kansas night was a beauty to behold. I never tired of admiring the glittering panorama of stars against a sky black as the hair of a Kiowa maiden.

I took the last shift, circling the camp until the Big Dipper in the northern sky signaled it was time to rouse everyone out. At the same time, Elijah's fire blazed, casting out shards of light into the darkness.

I rode through camp, calling out, "Let's go, ladies. Texas is waiting. Moving out in thirty minutes."

Lanterns flicked on throughout the camp—dull, yellow glows suffusing through the duck canopies of the emigrant wagons, reminding me of those Chinese lanterns I had once seen out in San Francisco.

Shadowy figures rolled out of the wagons, disappearing into the gray morning. Moments later, the ghostly bulks of oxen began materializing.

I reined up at Elijah's fire and dismounted, hitching Blue to a wagon wheel. The coffee was boiling, and the aroma filled the air with a rich, pungent tang. After three long hours nurse-maiding animals, I was ready for a jolt of Arbuckle's coffee.

Suddenly, a long, drawn-out scream split the darkness, a piercing shriek that diminished into a keening wail that screeched the word, "snake, snake, snake!"

A cold hand clutched my heart. Shucking my six-gun, I raced through the camp. A crowd was gathering around Maude Perkins' wagon. The rotund woman grunted as she dragged Matilda Schaefer over the wagon seat into the hands waiting below.

She saw me and pointed to the wagon bed. "In there. In the blankets."

The pale lantern cast twisted shadows over the agony and pain contorting the young woman's face. She clutched her forearm to her breast.

"You be careful," I yelled at Maude.

"Don't worry about me. Just kill that blasted snake."

My fingers fumbled with the iron hooks holding the tailgate, but finally, I freed them. I held the gate for a moment, wondering if the reptile was just waiting for it to open. Some of the ladies had gathered behind me. "Back away. Now."

They didn't have to be told twice.

I released the tailgate and jumped back, bringing my Colt up to fire.

The flickering lantern cast shadows into the corners of the wagon bed. All I saw were ominous patches of darkness among the quilts and blankets.

Grabbing a Moses' Stick, I fished the top blanket out. Nothing. I licked my lips. My throat was so dry I couldn't swallow.

Somewhere I heard women crying, moaning, praying, but all I had on my mind was that snake. I fished another blanket from the wagon.

Still nothing.

By now, the Colonel, Lay, and the wranglers had gathered, all offering different suggestions. Ignoring them, I slid the Moses' Stick beneath the blankets, thinking that might stir up a reaction. It did.

One of those rattlers decided to vacate his bed, and at a full chisel.

I heard Maude shout, "Here he comes." But by the time she said it, the rattlesnake had lunged from the tailgate, all five feet of him striking the ground a good six feet distant. I spotted him as a blur and leaped aside. Fortunately, he was in the air and did not have the leverage to twist enough to strike at me.

"Don't shoot," I shouted. "Don't shoot." As clustered together as we were, someone would have been hit.

I needn't have said anything, for everyone behind me had scattered and was running in every direction. He hit the ground. I threw up my Colt, expecting him to coil and strike, but he didn't stop. Throwing one blurring loop after another, he quickly disappeared into the shadowy sage of the graying morning.

Peering back into the wagon, I saw Maude standing on the seat. She sighed. "At least, he's gone." She glanced around at the group of women below her. "I'll get some bandages," she said, stepping into the bed.

"Out!"

She looked at me in surprise. "What?"

"Out! Get out of there. There might be others."

She stared at me a moment, then the roly-poly woman jerked her foot back.

Easing the Moses' Stick back under the blankets, I dragged the rest of them onto the ground.

"Look!" Maude shouted. "Two more."

Coiled in one corner of the wagon bed were two smaller snakes, their rattles suddenly humming like a swarm of angry bees.

Lay raised his Colt, but I stopped him. "The slug will ricochet. Hold on." I scooted the lantern to the end of the wagon. "Maude. Grab a lantern and dump coal oil on them. That'll drive 'em out."

She did, and moments later, the last two rattlesnakes slithered from the wagon and disappeared into the tall grass around the camp. I handed Lay the Moses' Stick. "Make sure there's not any more hiding in the blankets."

Up front, the Colonel was tending Matilda. The rattler had caught her under her forearm, driving his fangs deep into the soft flesh.

Elijah limped up. "Here, Colonel." He handed the Colonel a small bag. "Snakeroot. Instead of tobacco. My Mama used it on the plantation."

Colonel Egerton lanced the bites and extracted as much venom as he could. He packed the wound as Elijah instructed. He looked up at the ladies. "You can put her back inside now. Keep her quiet. We'll change the packing in a hour or so." He rose and dusted his jeans. I thought I saw a grimace of pain on his face, but when I looked again, it had vanished, or maybe I had imagined it.

Elijah said, "Make a potion. Best she takes two–three doses a day. It do stop the poison."

The young woman lay moaning on the ground, her pale and sweaty face twisted in pain, her lips drawn in thin lines over her teeth. Effortlessly, Bertha Lewis lifted Matilda and laid her in the arms of two women in the back of the wagon.

By now the sun had risen. Colonel Egerton sidled up beside me. "She won't make it. He was a big one."

I was sick to my stomach. "What if we got her back to town?"

He shook his head. "I don't figure that would help. He put a heap of poison in that little lady."

The idea of just waiting for her to die stuck in my craw. I went over to the wagon. "Miss Matilda?"

Katherine Stanton was one of the women in the wagon with Matilda. Both women looked at me. Matilda kept her eyes closed against the pain.

"Miss Matilda," I said again. "We need to take you back to Westport. I'll put you on my pony with me and get you back where you can get proper care." I looked up at Katherine. "Get her ready," I ordered her.

A frail gasp stopped me. "N . . . No." Then it grew stronger. "No."

I stared in surprise at the thin woman. She was no bigger than a matchstick. "But, we don't have the medicine to do right by you."

She opened her eyes and stared at me. She struggled for breath. Katherine leaned forward and gently brushed the strands of damp hair from Matilda's sweaty forehead. "Please don't. This . . . This is my chance for . . ." She shut her eyes against another spasm of pain. Slowly, she relaxed and opened her eyes. "I'll die first," she gasped out.

All I could do was gape at her.

Chapter Six

The silence of the early morning hung over us so thick a jasper could reach out and touch it.

I jumped when a voice right behind me spoke up. "Well, you heard her, Ramrod. Now, let's get going."

I looked around and stared up at Bertha Lewis. There was a resolve in her eyes that made me wonder if I had been wrong about these ladies. I looked back at Matilda. Her arm had begun to swell. I shook my head. It was her call. "Alright, ladies. Let's head south." I turned to Katherine Stanton. "You best look after Miss Matilda."

For a woman even in the best of health, emigrant wagons were rougher than a ten-day journey over a corduroy road, but for someone snake bit, the pain had to be unbearable. But not once did she scream out.

By noon, her arm was the size of a watermelon, the

47

skin taut as a drumhead. Blood and poison continued to seep from the incisions, staining the blankets below her darkly. The ladies kept changing the bandages, applying fresh snakeroot.

We moved south as one, and as one we carried Matilda Schaefer in our minds. Despite the rigors of the journey, none of us could keep from questioning the bad luck that put her in the proximity of the rattlesnakes, and the good luck that kept the serpents from our own beds.

Mid-afternoon, the Colonel pulled up beside me. "She's unconscious. I think the arm might need lancing. Otherwise, the skin'll split."

I wondered about Elijah's snakeroot. It didn't seem to be too effective.

Throughout the afternoon, Elijah had been pulling off to the side and dismounting from his wagon. He was gathering weeds. Once, I rode over to him. He looked up and grinned, displaying a handful of weeds with spiked white tops. "Snakeroot. Young and tender. Good medicine."

"Well," I muttered skeptically as I rode back to the wagons. "Now I can say I've seen snakeroot."

That evening, we gathered around our fires in silence. Lay reported on the unconscious woman. "The arm looks bad. I think there might be some gangrene."

Gangrene? With snakebite, gangrene does set in fast, but not this fast.

A small group of women came toward us. Out of habit, we rose. Katherine Stanton stepped forward.

"Mister Forrest, what are you going to do about Matilda?"

"I offered this morning to take her back. I don't see there's much we can do except make her comfortable until . . ." I hesitated. My ears burned. "Well, you know what I mean. She got a big dose. And she's a mighty frail woman."

Maude Perkins rolled forward. "She won't go back, Mister Howie. She'd rather die than go back."

Elijah hobbled forward. "She don't die from the snake. The medicine, it takes care of the poison in the heart. That's what my Mama tolds me. It allus be that way, but that don't mean it won't kill other parts of the body. You needs to take her arm."

I studied him. I didn't believe one word he said. Oh, I know he believed what he said, but those were just folk superstitions. I looked back at the ladies, their faces taut with anxiety. There was no sense in amputating the arm. Matilda was probably going to die anyway.

Bertha spoke up. "The arm has got to go, Mister Howie. Will you do it?"

I looked up into her eyes, then down at the other ladies. They all stared at me hopefully. I looked around at the Colonel. He said nothing, but from the expression on his face, I knew we shared the same idea.

"First off, ladies," I replied. "Matilda doesn't have a ghost of a chance with all the poison in her system. I got no faith in snakeroot, though I am surprised she's still alive. Now, I know that sounds cruel, but I don't mean it that way. I just hate to cause her any more pain. If she insists, then I'll do it, but you got to understand how I feel about it."

Katherine shook her head. "I don't know about the medicine Elijah gave her, but the truth is, I thought she would be hurting more than she is now. Personally, I believe his snakeroot is helping, at least with the pain. You know the rot in her arm will kill her even if the poison doesn't. She needs a chance. You can give it to her."

I drew a deep breath, then released it. "All right. Let me take a look."

Snakebite was nothing new to me. I'd seen several, but none as ugly as this one, and in such a short time. The flesh around the wound was dying.

"Alright." I rolled up my sleeves. "Boil some water. Get clean rags. I'll put an edge on my knife. And here," I added, reaching in the chuck wagon and pulling out a bottle of Old Crow. "Get her drunk."

"And more snakeroot. The new root. I boiled up a tonic." Elijah nodded to the pot in the edge of the coals.

I shrugged. I didn't figure it would hurt the poor woman any more than what she was going through now. "Go ahead and mix the snakeroot tonic with the whiskey." Might as well get her good and drunk, I figured.

Thirty minutes later, I knelt beside Matilda in the wagon bed. Three lanterns had been hung from the hoops. She had dutifully downed a tin cup of snakeroot tonic and whiskey. She made a mumbling joke about how it tasted like hog slop. Everyone laughed.

She wore a silly grin on her face. The whiskey was working.

Her bare arm had been washed clean. An axe head had been placed in the fire to seal the cut. Elijah had provided a cup of powdered snakeroot for the wound.

Four ladies knelt by Matilda to hold her down.

Sweat stung my eyes. I sat back on my heels, unable to believe I was actually going to amputate another human being's arm.

I'd seen it done once down in South Texas when a brushpopper got his arm tangled in a rope drawn tight between a dead horse and an ornery longhorn. His arm was black as midnight, and no more than a few squirts of blood came out.

I looked into Matilda's eyes, wishing I had a few petals of the Apache drug, mescal. Beads of perspiration stood out on her pale face. She gave me a faint, tipsy grin. I glanced at the bottle of whiskey. Almost half empty. I hoped that was enough.

Glancing at Bertha, I nodded. She slipped a twisted roll of cloth between Matilda's teeth. "Bite down on it, honey," she whispered, tightening her fingers around Matilda's shoulder. The other ladies held her tightly.

"Bite hard," I said, flexing my sweaty fingers around the butt of the knife. The swollen, dark skin was taut; the rotting flesh was only a few inches from her elbow. That's where I'd make the cut, just below the elbow. Take off the bad flesh plus another inch or so. That way, she would at least have some use of the arm. If she lived, I reminded myself.

Gripping her forearm, I looked into her eyes once more. They were squeezed tight against the anticipated pain. I hoped she would faint and not have to endure the ungodly suffering. Taking a deep breath, I wiped my sleeve across my eyes once again, and made the first cut. Her arm erupted from the incision. Blood serum and pus squirted on my hands and arms.

The frail woman shrieked. Her body stiffened, rising off the wagon bed except for her shoulders and heels. "Hold her," I barked. "Don't let her move." For a moment, I thought she might break loose, but abruptly, she went limp.

I kept my throat closed and worked quickly. As soon as I reached the bone, a handsaw appeared. I glanced at Katherine.

She took the knife from my hand and gave me the saw. "It's clean," she whispered.

I drew a deep breath and sawed the bone. Then I seared the stump with the red-hot axe head and washed the wound with whiskey and then powdered it with Elijah's snakeroot.

With a sigh, I sat back. Katherine quickly wrapped the stump while Bertha bathed the unconscious woman's face gently. "Well, it's done."

I climbed out of the wagon. Behind me, a frail voice whispered. "Will she live?"

All I could do was shrug. "I don't know. Depends. She's got grit. If that's all it takes, I'd say she'd be fine, but the poison is in her blood. I'd be surprised if she lasted the night."

Katherine jerked around and glared at me. "You're just full of hope and charity, aren't you?"

Her sudden vehemence rocked me back on my heels. My cheeks burned. "Look, lady. I don't lie to myself, if that's what you mean. And I don't lie to others. I'm not going to tell you something I don't believe just to keep from hurting your female feelings."

Angrily, I wiped the bloody knife on my denims and jammed in back in its scabbard. I stormed back to my fire.

Chapter Seven

The stars in the Milky Way were so thick it looked like a broad white road sweeping across the raven black sky. I was right glad when my shift came around, for I had not been able to sleep. On the trail only two days, and it seemed like two months.

To my surprise, Matilda was still breathing the next morning. Bertha reported that the young woman had even managed to down some corn mush and coffee, and that her stump seemed to be healing well. There were no signs of infection.

Colonel Egerton clapped his hands and whooped. "Looks like we got luck on our side, Howie."

I grinned. "Seems like." But I wasn't ready to proclaim that Christmas was here. We had a long piece to travel, and we would need all the luck we could get.

The Colonel's words were not prophetic.

For the next few days, we had more trouble than a field full of locusts. Ladies strayed from the trail and busted wheels. One forgot to fasten the wagon tongue to the ring in the lead yoke and snapped the tongue in half. And every night, tempers flared, sometimes erupting into hair-pulling, nail-scratching fights I had to break up. We even lay over one day while four of the ladies recovered from eating some bad food.

That was the first time Virginia Lea Miller and the three other ladies approached me. "We want to go back to Westport, Mister Forrest," she announced.

I shook my head. "Too late, ladies. You're stuck with us until Fort Gibson."

They pitched a fit and promptly ran Colonel Egerton down. He stuck with me, not that it would have mattered, for I was ramrod, and there was no way I'd take wranglers from the train to escort four whining women back to Westport.

On the other edge of the sword, Matilda improved daily.

Regardless of our problems, we arose each morning, journeyed to evening, managed to survive the night, and did it all over again the next day.

We crossed the Cygnes River where three ladies panicked and let their wagons float downriver. We spent an extra day hauling the wagons back and fishing two ladies from dead trees in the middle of the river.

Homer managed to bog their wagon in mud, which took another half-day to free.

Two days later, we had a streak of luck and crossed the Little Osage without losing wagons or women or Homer bogging anything down. That night we camped on the south bank of the Little Osage, and I announced to the ladies that we all deserved a day of rest.

I didn't tell them they were all on edge and needed a break. I figured they knew.

No one argued.

In fact, one of the ladies pulled a battered accordion from her gear, and an impromptu hoedown was held. The ladies danced with each other as the wranglers looked on, itching to take part, but dutifully remembering my instructions about no consorting with the ladies.

A small contingent of ladies led by bouncy Maude Perkins implored me to relent just for the night. Reluctantly, I agreed.

Colonel Egerton leaned toward me as we watched them all dancing around in the firelight. Even Lay was taking part in the soiree. "One time won't hurt nothing, Howie."

I sipped some of Elijah's six-shooter coffee. "I hope you're right, Colonel."

The ladies were dancing the wranglers into the ground. I couldn't help noticing that Cole Haywood, that young one with the shoulder-length, sun-bleached hair was doing his very best to keep up with a young woman by the name of Judith Brooks and a second one named Lena Hudson. I grinned to myself. The boy was asking for trouble.

Sometime later, the Colonel nudged me in the ribs. "Take a look yonder."

Her arm still bandaged, Matilda Schaefer appeared at the rear of her wagon. Two wranglers rushed to help her down. She smiled shyly and sat in a straight-backed chair one of the ladies had brought out for her.

"Now that's a sight," the Colonel whispered. "A dandy sight."

I agreed. "I didn't think she'd make it." I glanced at Elijah. "I reckon that old man knows a heap more than all of us put together."

The Colonel chuckled. "I've knowed that for years, Howie."

"Just how old do you reckon he is?"

"Beats me. He looked like that forty years ago when I was a wet-eared fifteen-year-old."

"Escaped slave?"

"Never asked. Free man as far as I'm concerned. Told me once though that his daddy had been brought over on a ship. Reckon it was a slave ship, but I never asked no questions. He's a good man and a good friend. Part of the family."

I remained up long after the entire camp had turned in. With a cup of six-shooter coffee in my hand, I strolled outside of camp, staring far off into a darkness so complete a jasper couldn't tell which was sky and which was land.

From time to time, the night wrangler passed. Once

or twice, a coyote came close, curious of the dark object standing so still in the night. A hunting snake passed near. I didn't see him, but I could hear the sandy shuffling he made as he slithered over the prairie floor.

I gazed south and took a deep breath. Yep, I sure hoped a day off would put us all back in shape.

The next day was a lazy day except for Lay and Elijah. On the orders of the Colonel, Lay had ridden out before sunrise and bagged a deer. Elijah was to roast the haunches, backstrap, and ribs as well as bake a pile of sourdough biscuits and boil a pot of red-eye gravy for the evening meal.

All in all, the day was a good one.

As our habit, we pushed out before sunrise the next morning. If we didn't have any broken wheels, lost wagons, or snapped tongues, we'd reach Oklahoma Territory in seven or eight days and follow the Neosha River on down to Fort Gibson.

Traveling would become more difficult, for our trail wound through the edge of the Ozarks. The region was made up of moderate hills with clear, swift streams and steep-sided river valleys. The divides between the valleys were broad and flat.

I hoped we didn't have any more problems before reaching Oklahoma Territory because once we got into the Ozark foothills, I knew we'd have more than our share of busted wheels among the rocks and boulders along the trail.

The first two days after leaving the Little Osage

were uneventful. Nothing broke. No one got themselves lost. No one argued. I noticed the Colonel didn't seem as perky and full of energy as he had been, but I figured it was just the journey taking its toll on him like it had everyone else.

By the third night, I was feeling pretty smug. Every soul seemed to be cooperating. No fights, nothing lost or broken, and no one taking ill. We were making good time, and Elijah was keeping the coffee hot.

I drifted off to sleep, counting ox-drawn wagons and chattering females.

During the early morning hours, my eyes popped open. Something had awakened me. I lay motionless, my ears tuned to the night sounds. Then I heard it again. Snatches of voices, faint. Not the calming voice of the nighthawk. It was something else.

I looked around the camp. There was no moon, but the stars lit the countryside with an eerie blue glow.

Nothing appeared amiss. I arose and poked around. One of the wrangler's bedrolls was empty. I glanced at the other sleeping cowpokes. Joe Allen was riding herd. Emmett lay with his head on his saddle, his jaw slack and mouth agape. I accounted for all except Cole Haywood. I remember how on the night of the hoedown he had danced the evening away with Judith Brooks and Lena Hudson.

Suppressing the urge to blister the air with curses, I peered toward the dark wagons, hoping my suspicion was unfounded.

I crept outside the camp and listened.

At night on the prairie, campfires can be seen for miles, attracting all sorts of undesirables. I always made it a point to camp in a basin. The rolling hills surrounding the camp hid the fire for the most part.

Bits and pieces of the nighthawk's soothing voice came from the far side of the camp. I hoped I was wrong. Cole Haywood had proved a good hand, but if he had sneaked one of the ladies out of camp after I had warned them all, then I planned to jerk a knot in his tail and send him packing.

I dropped into a crouch and eased toward the crest of the hill, which was thick with shadows.

"Pssst!"

I froze and squinted at a dark shadow in a patch of some wild flowers. Cole Haywood turned his face toward me and motioned me to the ground. I started to speak out, but he gestured frantically beyond the crest.

"What is it?" I whispered, crouching at his side.

"I'm not sure. Something's out there. Visitors. Comancheros, maybe."

We peered over the crest.

Sure enough, several dark shadows appeared on the prairie. They were moving in our direction. Drifters? I didn't think so.

Anyone out skulking around so early in the morning was up to no good.

Cole jabbed his elbow in my side. "Over there. To the left."

Four more shadows appeared.

"Looks like eight or ten on horseback," I whispered.

" 'Bout what I figure."

"You watch. I'll wake the others. Scoot on back down first chance you get."

He shucked his handgun and nodded, keeping his eyes on the approaching shadows.

Quickly, I hurried back to the camp. After rousting out the Colonel and the wranglers, I awakened Katherine and Bertha and Maude. Katherine stared up at me, the starlight on her taut face revealing her fear. "Wake the others. Grab their Winchesters and hurry to the four wagons on the other side of the circle. Then tell them to crawl under the wagons. You ladies got Winchesters. Now, we'll see if you know what them Winchesters are for. Don't shoot at anything not on horseback."

"When do we shoot?" asked Katherine.

"You'll know."

Our plan was simple. We'd rig dummies in our soogans, then hide under the wagons on the far side of the camp. I sent Lay with Emmett to warn his brother. "And you boys stay out there with him and the herd. The animals'll get spooked when the gunfire starts."

I glanced at the darkness inside the wagons surrounding the glowing bed of coals that had been our fire. I crossed my fingers, reminding myself to lay low when the shooting started. I hoped the ladies wouldn't shoot each other.

Minutes later, Cole crawled in. "They should be coming over the top of the hill about now."

Chapter Eight

The night lay silent across the rolling hills. Crickets chirruped. An owl hooted. A second one replied. Whoever those jaspers out there were, they knew how to remain quiet.

I peered around the camp. Nothing moved.

Vague figures emerged from the shadows on the side of the hill. Abruptly, a rebel yell shattered the silence and the pounding of hooves thundered through the dying echoes of the cry.

With excited screams, half-a-dozen riders slashed through the wagons and fired upon the motionless bedrolls.

"Now!" I shouted.

A cannonade of rifle fire exploded. Orange bursts of fire lit the darkness, streaking across the clearing like hundreds of rockets criss-crossing in the night.

Horses bleated and reared. Men screamed and tumbled from the saddles, and still the gunfire continued. The owlhoots returned a few scattered shots. I heard frightened shouts from beyond the camp, the echoes of retreating hoofbeats that quickly faded.

Abruptly, another fusillade of gunfire erupted, then suddenly ceased.

Behind me, the animals milled about along with a few nervous bellows and fearful whinnies. I hoped the boys could keep the animals from stampeding.

The night grew silent. The only sound was the soft whisper of the breeze brushing across the top of the grass. One or two nickers came from the downed ponies. Moans carried through the night.

Rising slowly, I called out, "Stay inside, but keep ready."

Colonel Egerton followed. He was breathing heavy, but I paid no attention. I was worried about the jaspers on the ground before us.

Two ponies struggled to their feet and ran off into the night. Elijah stirred up the fire and hurried to us with a lantern.

Five owlhoots lay sprawled on the sandy ground, four dead, and one dying.

Their faces a mixture of fear and pride, the ladies gathered, eyeing the dead.

Lay came running in. He slid to a halt and stared at the men on the ground. "We got two out there. They come riding smack up on us. I reckon they was surprised, for their shots went wilder than a bobcat in a feed sack."

Slowly I holstered my handgun.

"Who do you reckon they were? Don't look like Comancheros to me." The Colonel knelt by one and fumbled in the dead man's shirt pocket. Just a bag of Bull Durham.

"Scavengers. Reckon they saw a train load of women and decided they were easy pickings." I nodded to Ed Dowling and Al Thigpen. "Grab some shovels. Let's put them under. I want to move out before sunrise."

A few of the ladies looked at me in surprise. I ignored them. We didn't have time to waste in camp. I couldn't tell if any of the scavengers had escaped or not. For all I knew, there could be fifty of them heading for us at that very moment.

We pushed out.

At noon, the storm hit, a driving rain that cut visibility to less than a hundred feet. After a few minutes, the pelting rain let into a steady drizzle that continued for the next three days.

The second night of the rain, the good behavior of the ladies fell apart.

Elijah had rigged a fly from the chuck wagon so we could eat out of the rain. The Colonel had climbed into his soogan under the wagon. Lay and me were sitting cozy out of the rain, sipping six-shooter coffee when we heard loud voices.

The intensity of the voices increased, and suddenly shrill shrieks cut through the drizzle. A cacophony of high-pitched screams filled the air.

Lay and I exchanged startled looks. We jumped to our feet and raced toward the commotion.

A lantern hung from the canopy of a wagon, and a crowd of ladies were gathered in the glow of the lantern. I pushed through and discovered two screaming, biting women rolling in the mud scratching and pulling each other's hair.

Had it been two men, I would have kicked both in the rear. I considered that option for a moment, but figuring there was some truth in the old saying that discretion was probably the better part of valor, I grabbed one in each hand and yanked them apart.

What I didn't know then, but I do now is that when women want to fight, they're going to fight—anyone.

They turned on me, hissing and clawing and spitting and kicking. "Hold on there," I yelled. I had all I could do keeping my hands on their foreheads in an effort to keep them away from me. I yelled at Lay, "Grab one of these women."

They were both covered with slippery mud from toe to head, which made them hard to hold. We grasped and grappled, and two or three times, one would pop loose from our grasp and attack whoever happened to be closest.

Finally, we got them under control. I held Lena Hudson at arm's length by the back collar of her dress. I looked at the chunk of mud Lay had wrapped his arms about. "Who you got there?"

The rain washed the mud from her face. It was Judith Brooks. Suddenly, I knew what was going on, but

I wanted to hear it from them. I shook Lena. "What's this all about?"

"None of your business!" She erupted like a cat coming out of a box, arms and legs going in every direction.

I knew how to handle that. Still keeping her at arm's length, I shoved her over to the water barrel, yanked off the top, and poked her head down in the water.

Giggles sounded behind me.

I counted to five and pulled her up. "You ready to tell me?"

"Go to—"

I poked her head back in, this time to a count of ten.

She came up sputtering and spewing. "Alright, alright. You're drowning me."

"Don't tempt me. Now, what's going on here?"

Lena twisted around so she could glare at me. Her muddy blond hair hung in thick strings over her face. Her dress sagged with layers of mud. She looked worse than what the proverbial cat dragged in.

The two women eyed each other malevolently. "It's personal," Judith Brooks hissed.

"She's right," Lena Hudson snapped. "It's personal."

I eyed both ladies, then studied the onlooking women. Several dropped their eyes, a subtle, but definite statement that I would get nothing from them.

The rain grew heavier. We were all soaked. "Personal don't go around here," I growled. "You got personal problems, you wait until we reach Palo Pinto. Then you settle them. You two understand me?"

They both glared at me.

Just to make sure they all understood, I added, "Ladies, you been sniping at each other ever since the second day out. A night doesn't pass that the two of you don't almost come to blows. Well, I'm making you a promise right now. No more fighting. Any more trouble and I'll drop the culprits off at Fort Gibson. You can fight to your heart's content there. If I have to toss every last one of you off the train, I'll do it. You understand?" I looked around at the crowd, my eyes daring anyone to say a single word.

The only response was a horde of icy glares.

"All right, ladies. Show's over. Get back in your wagons out of the rain. Don't want none of you getting sick on me."

"Why's that, Mister Forrest? Afraid we'll slow you down?" Katherine Stanton had stepped from the crowd. She stared at me defiantly.

I had no idea why we rubbed each other the wrong way, but we did. "That's right, Miss Stanton. I don't want no one slowing us down. Any of you ladies take sick or eat bad food, you'll have to keep on moving or get left behind."

I headed back to the chuck wagon with Lay. I gestured to Cole for him to follow me. We ducked under the fly and squatted against a wagon wheel while Elijah poured us some coffee.

The Colonel propped himself up on his elbow beneath the wagon and grunted. "You really going to do that, Howie?"

"Well, probably not, but they don't know it." I grinned sheepishly. "Them women, Colonel. Herding them is like trying to stuff an old tomcat in a box."

He chuckled and lay back down.

I turned to Cole. "I reckon you know what those two woman was fighting over?"

Lay cocked his head, curious as to what I had on my mind.

Cole stared at me with all the artlessness of a truly naïve young man. "Huh?"

I studied him a minute. Behind me the Colonel chuckled. Elijah looked on, a grin on his face. The young man honestly had no idea. He was dumber than I thought. "You. They were fighting over you."

Mouth agape, he stared at me. "Huh?"

Patiently, I explained. "You remember the other night when we had the hoedown and you danced with Judith Brooks and Lena Hudson?"

"Yep. What about it?"

"They're taken with you."

I watched the wheels start turning in his head. They were slow to start, but as they picked up momentum, a broad grin spread over his face. "Is that right? Them two ladies?"

"Yep."

He shook his head. "Well, whatta you know?"

Slowly, I pulled my knife from its scabbard. "See this blade?"

"Yeah. So?"

"So, I took it off a Union soldier in the War of Secession. Since then, I've taken half-a-dozen Injun scalps. You mess with either of those ladies, and I'll have yours. Savvy?"

Lay choked on his coffee.

Cole Haywood's eyes grew wide. He glanced at Elijah, who nodded his old head slowly as if to verify my threat. His Adam's apple bobbed once or twice. "Yes, sir. I savvy, but honest, Mister Forrest. I never had no mind about none of them. That's gospel."

I fixed my eyes on his, drawing my thumb over the edge of the blade. "I hope so, boy. I've come to tolerate you. Hate to see all that effort on my part go for nothing."

He sat his coffee down hard, splashing it on the ground. "Don't worry none at all, Boss. I promise."

"Good." I nodded. "I'm holding you to that."

After Cole was out of earshot, Elijah chuckled. "You ought to be ashamed of yourself, Mister Howie. Telling that poor white boy all them lies about you and that there knife."

"Well, Elijah, I don't really look at what I told him as a lie. It's really like one of those stories you tell someone to make a point. You know, like preachers do sometimes."

Lay laughed.

Chapter Nine

The rain continued throughout the night. I awakened once or twice shivering, but I snuggled down under my tarps and went back to sleep. When I climbed out for my shift with the stock, a spasm of shivers started my teeth clattering.

I clenched my teeth. After all my ranting and raving to the ladies about not stopping for anyone, I could not be sick. I would not be ill.

By the time my shift was over and the train was ready to pull out, I was sicker than a deacon with a two-day hangover. My head throbbed, my face burned, my muscles shivered, and my stomach kept turning over and over, but by all that was holy, we were moving out before sunrise even if I had to crawl.

Word quickly spread among the wagons. Throughout the morning, the ladies were all very generous in their offering of remedies that smelled bad enough to gag a dog on a gut wagon and greasy, spicy food that wouldn't lie still in even a cast-iron stomach.

When I declined, they returned to their wagons laughing. Some of those ladies had a cruel streak in them.

From candle-lighting to candle-lighting, that was the longest day I had ever spent. I jumped into my soogan right after supper and died. When I awakened before my shift, I was hungry, a good sign.

I choked down a small portion of beans and bread and went out to relieve Cole.

"You going to live?"

"Afraid so." I groaned.

And I did, but the next morning, Colonel Egerton didn't wake up.

When I rode in from the last shift, I spotted Elijah sitting next to the Colonel under the wagon. The old man's shoulders were slumped and shaking.

I tied up to a wagon wheel and ducked under the fly. I frowned. "What's going on?"

Elijah looked around at me. His eyes were red, and tears streamed down his dark face. "The Colonel, Mister Howie. The Colonel done died on me."

"What?" I stared in disbelief.

Elijah nodded. "He done died."

"He can't be." I crawled under the wagon and checked the Colonel's pulse, then pressed my ear against his chest. No pulse, no heartbeat.

His skin was cool.

I shivered.

Outside, the rain continued, a chilling drizzle pattering against the canvas fly with the steady, solemn beat of a funeral drum.

"Colonel!"

I jerked around to see Lay standing by the fire, staring in shock. His eyes met mine. I nodded.

"You sure?"

I nodded again. He stood woodenly for several moments. He closed his eyes briefly, his shoulders sagged, and then gestured to Al Thigpen. "Get the shovels. We got work to do."

With the ladies looking on, we buried the Colonel there in the sodden earth on the crest of a small rise. We left an iron yoke ring and a wooden marker, but I knew that within weeks, there would be no trace of a grave ever having been here.

I learned from Lay that the Colonel had given him explicit orders on what to do if such an incident took place. "He didn't want us to waste time, Howie. This here cargo of ladies meant ever'thing to him. He wants them back to Palo Pinto as soon as possible." He hesitated. "He knew this could happen."

Thinking back to that first day in the saloon, I remembered the Colonel telling me he had a bad heart. I shook my head. "It was one Sam Hill of a time for it to go out on him."

I glanced back over my shoulder at the rolling hills on the horizon. I told myself I could still see the yoke ring, but down deep, I knew I couldn't. Somehow, the rain grew colder and the clouds grew darker.

Finally, the rain ceased, and the sun came out. Steam rose from the soaked ground, enveloping us in a suffocating and sticky heat. Despite the hardships, the rain, the heat, the sun, the mud, no one complained. Maybe it was the threats I had made, or maybe it was that we all remembered the Colonel and the dreams he had died for.

That night, Bertha Lewis stopped by the chuck wagon with a bowl of steaming broth. "I always made this up for my late husband when he was puny, Mister Howie. It should perk you up."

I thanked her. She gave me a shy smile and returned to her own campfire. The broth was delicious, and minutes later, I dropped off to sleep.

When I awakened for the last shift on the herd, I felt like a new person. Elijah propped himself up on an elbow. "How you feeling this morning, Mister Howie?"

I laughed and pulled on my boots. "Well, Elijah, I feel like the biggest toad in the puddle this morning. That's exactly how I feel."

Throughout the day, the countryside grew rougher. "Close to Indian Territory," I muttered to Lay, who had been riding at my side. I gestured to the dark line of mountains on the eastern horizon. "Soon we'll reach the foothills of the Ozarks."

"This the trail you took coming up?"

"Not yet. Right soon, all this prairie will bottleneck between a couple ranges of mountains. Not real mountains like the Rockies or the Smokies, but they'll be mountains enough for our wagons. That's where we'll strike the Neosha River and follow it in to Fort Gibson and the Arkansas River. We can lay over there a few days and let the animals rest."

Behind us, the tiny wagon train wound over and around rolling sandstone hills. Mesquite and cedar scrub was beginning to appear, and far to the southwest, a line of trees marked the Neosha River.

Two days later, we hit the cattle trail I'd taken from the Red River up to Westport. Less than half-a-day's journey ahead was the welcoming shade of the sweet gum and hickories lining the Neosha.

The foothills grew rougher. Dark, angular slabs of granite projected from thin soil, forming perpendicular walls that stretched to the horizon. It reminded me of a jigsaw puzzle with the pieces jammed into the wrong slots. Vegetation erupted from the fissures between the ill-fitting slabs.

Lay and I rode up beside Elijah. The old greasybelly nodded to the river. "We going to make an early stop, Mister Howie?"

For a moment, I considered the question. I drawled. "Naw. We still got a couple hours. Pick up another mile or so." I glanced back over the train. As much as I hated to admit it, the ladies had proven equal to the task—so far.

I spotted Katherine Stanton striding beside her

wagon. Matilda Schaefer walked alongside the second wagon. Her strength was slowly returning and now she managed to walk six or so miles daily. She was one catawamptious surprise to me. By all rights, she should have died that first day.

I was beginning to believe the Colonel had passed along his grit and determination to the ladies—all except Virginia Lea Miller and her party of whiners. I couldn't wait for Fort Gibson so we could leave them behind.

Bertha's wagon was last. She'd make any jasper a fine wife. Of course, I couldn't help grinning to myself that she'd probably end up with a sawed-off runt whose sombrero came only to her shoulders.

"Keep your fingers crossed, Lay, that things keep rocking along like they are." I grinned at him.

He grinned back. A sad look came over his face. "The Colonel would sure be proud."

For a moment, thoughts of the Colonel overcame the exuberance I was feeling. "Yeah. Reckon you're right. It's tough losing someone like that. But figure it this way, Lay. You're carrying out his last dream. He'd be mighty happy."

The young man chewed on his bottom lip, then sighed. "Reckon you're right, Howie. The Colonel's gone. He ain't coming back." He looked up at me. "You know, I never knew my folks or family. This is the first time I ever lost anyone close to me. It sure is an unsettling feeling. Like you're missing something inside, and you can't quite figure out what."

I nodded. I knew the feeling.

* * *

That night we camped on the banks of the Neosha, a smooth-flowing, gently curving river that looked like it came straight out of a picture book.

Like all boys, Homer Jackson raced up and down the riverbank, pausing to skip stones across the surface. Except for bogging a wagon at the Cygnes River, the young boy had caused no trouble. But, we had a long way to still go.

The atmosphere in camp that night was almost festive. Even Katherine Stanton relaxed. At least, when she brought us a pot of stew, she didn't throw it on me.

She handed it to Elijah. "We decided you didn't need to cook tonight, Elijah. You can rest with the other men."

Our eyes met when she said "men." I would have sworn I saw a mocking gleam in her eyes.

"Thank you, ma'am. I's much obliged," replied Elijah, setting the pot on a rock at the edge of the coals.

The wranglers nodded deferentially. "Thank you, ma'am," they muttered.

Katherine hesitated, glancing around the camp. Giant hickories and maple spread their limbs above us, forming a green canopy lit by the firelight. "It's so good to put all of those boring sand hills behind us." She gestured to the river. "At least we can look at something different for a spell."

I agreed. But I kept quiet about the rigors of the trail ahead. By the time we reached the Red River, she'd be begging for those boring sand hills. We were entering the Ozark foothills and from them, we had to cross the Ouachita Mountains in the southeastern part of Indian Territory.

She spoke to Lay. "What's it like in Palo Pinto?"

A broad grin spread over the young cowpoke's face. "Like the Colonel claimed. A Garden of Eden. Good graze. Cold sweet water in the streams. Fertile soil. And enough land for everyone."

Katherine gave me a sidelong glance before asking her next question. "What about you, Lay? You have a girl back in Palo Pinto?"

Despite his sun-darkened skin, you could see the blood rise in his cheeks. He ducked his head. "No, ma'am. Seems like I never had time."

The wranglers snickered.

She laughed, a bright, gay tinkle like Christmas bells. "Well, there's plenty here who think you're a charmer."

His blush deepened.

The wranglers chuckled aloud, and I tried to keep from grinning at Lay's discomfort. Katherine spotted me and added, "You needn't grin, Mister Howie. Believe it or not, there are one or two crazy women here who think the same about you."

The wranglers howled in delight.

Her words threw me into confusion. I didn't know whether she had paid me a compliment or an insult. I just shrugged and kept my mouth closed.

She tossed her head. "Well, I need to get back to the wagon. There's women's work to be done." She shot me a knowing look and spun on her heel.

"Hey, Howie." Cole Haywood laughed. "How do it feel to be a charmer?"

The others cackled like fat hens.

"I don't know," I shot back. "Why don't you ask Lay here? He can tell you."

Lay's ears burned. He yanked off his sombrero and slapped my shoulder with it. "You talk too much, you know it?"

We all laughed, and then headed for the pot of stew.

If I'd known what lay ahead, I might not have laughed so hard.

Chapter Ten

The night was silent and dark. The cattle milled lazily, contented. False dawn lit the sky to the east. My shift was almost over when shouts erupted in camp. I muttered under my breath, "Now what in the blazes has happened?"

Lay came riding out. "Howie. Hey, Howie. Homer's gone. His Ma went looking for him when she got up, and he was gone."

By now, voices from the camp were calling the boy's name.

Eyes swollen, face taut with fear, Nelly Jackson wrung her hands and stared up at me. "I heard him coughing earlier, but when I got up a few minutes ago, he wasn't under the wagon where he usually sleeps." She pressed her fists against her lips.

79

"We searched the camp. He's nowhere around," said Katherine.

"Maybe he's over at the canoe," Maude Perkins volunteered.

As one, we stared at her.

My jaw dropped open. "Canoe? What canoe?"

A perplexed frown knit her forehead. "Why, the one he found just after we camped. It has a hole in it." She looked at Nelly curiously. "Didn't he tell you about it last night?"

Nelly's eyes grew wide with consternation. "No. How'd you know?"

Maude shrugged. "I saw him when I was gathering wood for the fire."

A chill ran down my spine. "Just where was this canoe?"

"Upriver. At the bend."

At the bend, I found Homer's sign, brogan tracks in the mud. Both the tracks and the skid mark of the canoe stern led into the water. "Here's where he went in," said Lay. "And look," he added, pointing to a pile of rags and the grease bucket farther up on the bank.

I muttered a curse to myself. The blasted boy had tried to patch the canoe. I looked out across the river. No sign of him.

Nelly cried out. "Oh, dear Lord, no. Not Homer. Not my child. Please, don't take him." Her eyes rolled back in her head, and she collapsed. The other ladies hurried to her.

"Get her back to her wagon," I said. "We'll search

the river. Cole, you come with Lay and me. Emmett, you boys take care of the stock. We'll be back later."

Throwing the saddles on our ponies, we headed downriver. Cole spoke up from behind. "How do you read it, Howie?"

"Depends on how good a job he did on the patch. It probably didn't hold for long. I just hope the boy can swim."

We rode slowly, studying the near and far shorelines.

"I don't reckon he could have gone too far," Lay said, indicating the slow, smooth current of the river.

Two miles downriver, we came upon the bark canoe, washed ashore on its side. A gaping hole near the stern grinned up at us crookedly, but what caught our attention was an arrow that had penetrated the bow and stuck in one of the thwarts.

Cole cursed. We stared at each, each refusing to speak of the fate we were all certain Homer had met.

I motioned downriver. "The two of you search this shore for tracks. I'll look for some sign on the far shore." With a click of my tongue, I urged my dun into the cool water. Within a few feet, he was swimming. The smooth current was deceptively strong, pushing us downriver. If Homer had capsized midriver, he could have been carried a far piece downstream.

After a few minutes, my pony touched bottom and scrambled ashore. The current had swept me almost half a mile below Lay and Cole. I waved. They waved back.

The gravel and mud shoreline made tracking simple, but I found nothing except animal and bird sign. Mid-morning, a shout from across the river caught my attention.

Cole was waving frantically while Lay knelt, studying the shore. A wave of relief washed over me when I realized that at least the boy hadn't drowned.

I drove the dun into the river.

"Cherokee, you think?" Cole Haywood rested his hand on the butt of his six-gun while he scanned the thickets around us.

Ears forward, our ponies stutter-stepped nervously when they picked up the Indian scent.

The sign was obvious. Brogan tracks suddenly surrounded by unshod pony tracks, all filled with water. Homer had turned to run, but ponies had cut him off. In a small, damp patch of earth was the perfect imprint of a moccasin.

"Cherokee? I don't think so. Kiowa probably. This is their country."

Lay held his pony under a tight rein. "You have any Injun trouble on the drive up?"

The tracks led east, toward the rugged Ozarks. "Nope. Saw a few, but they never came near."

"How many here, do you figure?"

I rode along beside the trail of the small party. The hoof prints grew farther apart. The small party was moving fast. "Four, maybe five."

Cole rode up beside me. "There's three of us. What

are we waiting for? Let's run them down and get the boy back."

"Not so fast," Lay said. "We don't want to take a chance on the boy getting hurt."

"Don't worry about that." I shook my head. "Most Indians, including the Kiowa, take young boys for adoption."

"Adoption?" Cole frowned at me.

Taking care to stay to the side of the trail, I replied, "Yep. You see, most tribes today have a shortage of young men. Warring tribes and Federal troops have planted a heap of fighting warriors in the ground."

Lay reined up. "What do we do now?"

I studied the situation. "Hard to say. The Kiowa are torn between Big Tree and Kicking Bird. Kicking Bird wants peace. Big Tree, war." I shook my head. "I don't figure this is a war party. Could be a small band carrying a peace belt."

The younger man stared at the sign at our feet. "Peace with who?"

"That's tricky. Could be the Jicarilla Apache back west or maybe Arapaho or Cheyenne to the north."

"You can't say for sure, though." Cole's eyes fixed mine defiantly. "This could have been the remains of a war party."

"Could be." I shrugged. "Truth is, just from the sign, a jasper can't tell what tribe even. But, I'm wagering they were Kiowa." I reined up and stared over the trail leading across the rugged countryside. "You boys go back to the train. Follow the Neosha to Fort Gibson. Wait for me."

Lay's face grew grim. "You can't go by yourself."

"That's the best way. Shows courage. Indians respect courage. Besides, the wagon train has to get to Texas. That's more important than either the boy or me. Wait at Fort Gibson a week. If I'm not back, head south to the Santa Fe Trail, then take the Texas Trail to the Red. From there, you won't have any trouble reaching Jacksboro."

Reluctantly, Lay agreed. He nodded to my sidearm. "You got plenty ammunition? Maybe you ought to come back to camp and pack some grub."

"Nope. I got my canteen and a bag of jerky. I'll get more if I need it. They're moving fast. Once they get up in those rocky hills, they'll be harder to track than a grasshopper over gravel." I checked my cartridges while I spoke. I had a full belt and an extra box in my saddlebags. "Yep," I added. "I got enough of everything." I wheeled the dun about. "Look after them ladies."

The small party were only four. I followed the sign at a gallop, slowing only when we crossed rocky ledges. They headed due east, up into the Ozarks, making no effort to hide their trail.

And that puzzled me. At the same time, I felt some reassurance of my first guess that the small band was on a peaceful mission. Otherwise, they would be a heap more sneaky in their travel than they were.

The countryside grew rugged, the soil thin. The trail wound through multi-layered slabs of granite, around sinkholes filled with water, under fragmented upthrusts from which cold, clear water gushed, splashing into glittering pools and carried down the mountainside in narrow, twisting streambeds.

At noon, I reined up on the rim of a sheer bluff. A basin of hardwoods, oak, hickory, maple, stretched to the next mountain miles to the east.

From the midst of the canopy of green, a tenuous thread of smoke drifted into the blue sky. They weren't more than an hour ahead.

With a click of my tongue, I urged the dun down a twisting trail that clung to the sheer face of the granite escarpment. I hoped the small party had a *topadok'i*, a camp leader. Older warriors usually exercised a cooler temper and wiser judgment than a handful of young bucks anxious to count coup.

"Take it easy, Blue," I whispered to my pony, laying my hand on his neck. "No hurry. They'll let us catch them soon enough."

An hour later, I rode into the basin and followed the obvious trail left by the small party. They knew I was following them. Mid-afternoon, I reined up as I approached a clearing. Through the tangle of undergrowth and leaves, I spotted the warriors astride their ponies facing the mouth of the trail from which I would enter the clearing.

I flipped the rawhide look from the hammer of my Colt. I hoped I wouldn't have to use it.

My pony pricked his ears forward. He tossed his head when he scented the Indian ponies. I rounded a bend in the trail and stepped into the clearing. I reined up.

Homer leaned from behind a young warrior and waved. "Howie."

A guttural remark from the warrior caused the boy to jerk his head back.

Immediately, I took in my situation. The clearing was less than thirty feet across. If they charged me, I could probably get two, maybe a third. If—

To my relief, an older warrior urged his pony forward a step or two. I dallied my reins about the saddle horn. I raised my right hand, but kept my left dangling near my Colt. "I am a friend. I do not come to fight."

The brave nodded. "You come for boy."

It was not a question, but rather a simple statement of fact. "Yes. It is as if the heart has been taken from his mother." I grimaced as soon as I spoke. It was the wrong thing to say.

He shrugged. "Women are weak."

The Kiowa were patriarchal. They cared nothing of a woman's feelings. I touched my fingers to my chest. "I have been raising the boy. He has no father. I have taken that place."

"Where were you when the boy went into the river last night? What father would permit such?"

"No father. He is like the Kiowa boy. Sometimes they do not listen. Their heads are like the rocks. But, I will beat him until he understands what he did wrong."

The warrior studied me a moment. A trace of a smile erased the frown on his face. Before he could speak, the warrior with Homer rode up beside the first brave. He glared at me. "Wind Whistle does not speak for me. I found the boy. I take him to my father who lost one his age during the last snows. I will not give him up."

I eyed the older warrior. "The young now speak for the *topadok'i*?"

He looked at me in surprise, shot a warning glare at the younger warrior, then turned back to me. "You know of our people?"

"Yes. I know the Kiowa to be honorable. Not thieves who sneak in the night and steal children." Of course, that was exactly what they did, but they didn't cotton to being reminded of it.

He turned to the younger warrior. I knew a few words of Kiowa jargon, but they spoke too quickly and with too much anger for me to make out what they were saying. Of course, I didn't have to hear. I knew exactly what was taking place. The young brave disputed the *topadok'i*'s demands. As unobtrusively as possible, I eased my right hand close to the butt of my Colt.

The reins were dallied around the saddle horn. My knees were locked around the dun's belly. If a melee exploded, I'd be right in the middle with both Colts.

The younger warrior glared at me, then reached behind him and yanked Homer from his pony. The young boy sprawled on the ground, but instantly bounced to his feet and sprinted to me.

Without taking my eyes off the angry warrior, I offered Homer my hand to swing up behind me.

I nodded briefly to the *topadok'i* and backed my dun down the trail and around the first bend. Instantly, I wheeled him around and raced back up the trail. Homer clung to me, his arms wrapped around my waist, his cheek pressed into my back. I didn't fool myself that the trouble was over.

Chapter Eleven

The sun dropped slowly in the west. The shadows cast by the mountains lengthened. Homer had spoken not a word.

We stopped on the rim of a sheer precipice over which a narrow stream tumbled thirty feet down the rugged face of the escarpment into a small pool in a narrow ledge before spilling over the edge and falling another two hundred feet to the rocks below.

Blue drank eagerly. Upstream from my pony, Homer and me filled our own bellies with the icy, sweet water. I handed the boy a strip of jerky. "Chew on this, boy. It'll fill the hole in your belly."

He looked up at me. "Are ... are we going to be okay, Mister Forrest?"

I gave him a crooked grin. "Just fine, Homer. Just fine." I looked out over the valley below. Somewhere far to the west the wagon train was putting up for the night. With luck, we'd reach them tomorrow.

But first, I had to make plans for the night. There was no doubt in my mind we would have some visitors.

When I turned back to my pony, a numbing blow slammed into my forehead. I stumbled back toward the rim. My eyes opened wide in surprise, and as a wave of darkness swept over me, the report of a heavy rifle echoed across the valley. I felt myself falling, and in the distance, I heard Homer scream.

Slowly, the sensation of water splashing on me elbowed its way into the recesses of my brain. With that came a gut-wrenching headache, a throbbing beat that threatened to take off the back of my skull.

I groaned and moved my head, right into a pool of icy water. I shivered, but remained motionless, letting the chilled water ease the pounding in my skull. After a few minutes, I moved my arm and froze. Slowly I wiggled my fingers. They touched nothing but air.

I tried to collect my thoughts, but the blow had scrambled them. I pulled my arm toward me a few inches until my fingers touched granite.

Darkness swept over me again. When I awakened, night had fallen across the mountains. I lay motionless. My first thoughts were of Homer, and then I became aware I was on the ledge below the rim of the escarpment.

Gingerly, I tried to judge the width of the ledge at my feet with my toe. Inches to the right, and my toe slipped off the ledge. I lay motionless, my face still in the icy water. I drew my head back and tried to roll back against the face of the escarpment.

Muscles groaned. I clenched my teeth against the anticipated pain of broken or fractured bones. To my relief, nothing appeared busted. I leaned back against the rugged wall, ignoring the shards of granite poking my back.

Next I knew, I was blinking against the rising sun.

Struggling to sit upright on the narrow ledge, I flexed my arms and legs in an effort to work out the cricks and kinks. My hands burned. I looked at them in surprise. The skin had been raked from my fingers and palms.

Probably from grabbing at the granite face as I fell. That was what must have kept me upright when I hit, although I wouldn't have damaged too much if I'd hit on my head. Only a dull-witted greenhorn would have stood up in plain sight on the rim.

I leaned forward and splashed water in my face. I recoiled sharply as the icy water stung the raw scratches on my hand. My head throbbed, and I touched my fingers to a lump on my forehead.

My reflection in the water showed an ugly gash across my right forehead. Another half inch, and a third of my skull would have been missing.

Craning my neck, I peered up at the rim. The granite face down which I had slid was a series of layered fractures with sharp edges. That was how I had ripped the skin from my hands.

Struggling to my feet, I studied the sheer wall above. It was not quite perpendicular. That's why I had not plummeted another two hundred feet. Holding to one of the outthrusts, I peered over the ledge. The face of the mountain below was the same as above, layers of fractures in the granite.

"Well, Howie, now what?" I muttered to myself darkly.

There was no choice. I didn't reckon a rope was going to drop down on me out of plain air, so if I got out, I was going to have to climb out myself. The small, granite projections would offer both hand- and footholds.

I hoped.

I could go thirty feet up, or two hundred down. I opted to go up. If I fell, I still had the narrow ledge on which I was standing to stop me.

Flexing my fingers to limber them, I took a deep breath and started up the nearly vertical face of the escarpment. Slowly, I eased upward, my body pressed against the granite, my fingers clutched at two-inch knobs of rock, and my toes jammed into narrow fissures. Five, then ten, finally fifteen feet. I paused to catch a breath. Sweat stung my eyes, but I dared not wipe at them in case I lost my precarious balance.

Behind, the sun beat down on the granite face of the mountain. I could feel the heat radiating from the granite.

Without warning, the startling whine of a rattlesnake cut through the silence. I froze. The angry hum of the rattler came from my left.

Slowly looking back over my shoulder, I still saw nothing, but the thrumming of the angry rattler continued. Where in the blazes was he? Then I realized he was back in one of the spider web of fractures marking the face of the granite wall.

My brain raced. I had no choice. I had to keep climbing.

Holding my breath, I eased to my right away from the sound, moving as imperceptibly as possible. Ten minutes later, I had moved three feet. I paused. The rattling did not seem to be as agitated as it had been. I reached for the next ledge, clenching my teeth against the pain of a strike, but it never came.

I continued my climb, moving horizontally for several more feet before ascending once again. Mister Rattler remained wherever he was, thrumming those rattles.

Grunting and gasping for breath, I strained to maintain a grip on the tiny granite knobs. Finally, I spotted the rim just above my head. I threw an arm up and sighed with relief when my fingers clutched the rim. I threw up the other hand and with a groan, pulled myself over the top and rolled onto my back, letting my arms fall at my side.

I closed my eyes in relief.

When I opened them, I was staring up into the eyes of the Kiowa *topadok'i*!

He stood straight and tall at my side, staring down without expression, a battered Winchester resting in the crook of his arm.

I started to grab my Colt, but hesitated. He could have killed me as soon as I rolled onto the rim, but he hadn't.

He squatted, and I noticed a lump on the side of his head. He glanced at the knot on my head. "You have luck. Standing Fox never good with rifle."

I climbed to my feet. "That's his bad luck," I replied, looking around us.

"I come alone," he said. "Standing Fox want boy." He touched his fingers to the knot on his head. "I, Wind Whistle, try to stop him, but one struck me without warning. When I wake, they gone."

"Why'd you come to me?"

"I fear they kill you. Wind Whistle want no trouble with whites. I believe as Kicking Bird. The only future for the Kiowa is with the white man. Standing Fox is son of my brother. He is young and listens not to his father."

I studied him a moment. He was ten, maybe fifteen years my senior. Manhood had matured his body, erasing the definition of the lanky muscle and taut sinew of the young bucks. "You know where they're headed?"

He gestured to the northeast. "Make summer camp in *Aux Arc*. Come winter, camp move back to territory."

I had been with the Indians enough to know that *Aux Arc* was their name for the Ozarks, the French expression accorded the rugged mountains by the early explorers.

"You'll take me to them?"

"Yes."

I looked into his open, level-set eyes. They were cold and gray and honest. I believed him. I'd never known of a treaty between white and Indian broken by the latter.

Despite his pony now having to carry double, we covered several miles before dark and made a cold camp that night, chewing on jerky and pemmican and washing it down with fresh, sweet water.

Next morning we pulled out with the sun.

Within minutes, he reined up.

"What's wrong?"

He peered to the north, then east in the direction the sign led. "Standing Fox not go to *Aux Arc.*"

"Well, I reckon we'll have to track them."

Wind Whistle grunted and turned the pony east.

I'd always considered myself a better than fair tracker, but tracking in the forest is a heap different than on the plains. Wind Whistle taught me a few lessons that day.

I learned how to determine the length of time leaves had been overturned, or how long a branch had been snapped, or a leaf of grass broken.

Mid-morning, as Wind Whistle leaned forward to study the trail, I spotted a fleeting shadow glide across the trail deeper into the forest.

"Up ahead," I whispered.

Obviously he had spotted whoever was before us, for his only movement was a short nod. He continued searching the trail, playing their game now.

I slipped my six-gun from the holster.

The sunlight filtered through the canopy of leaves, dappling the forest with shadows that played tricks with the eyes.

Was it the Kiowas ahead? And where was Homer? What if they'd tied him in some secluded hideaway that we could never find?

Without warning, Wind Whistle jerked around, slinging his elbow into me, carrying us both from the saddle. At the same time, he cried out. "Apache!"

Apache? I slammed to the ground on my back, at the same time shucking my handgun as a bull-shouldered warrior came over the croup of the Indian pony. Digging my heels in the soft humus ground cover, I shoved backward, at the same time pumping off two quick shots.

The slugs caught the fierce warrior in the chest, knocking him aside. Too busy to pay attention to Wind Whistle, I rolled to my right and jumped to my feet just as another fired at me. His slug caught my sleeve. I dropped to a knee and fired four times, the impact of each knocking him backward a step.

As suddenly as the attack started, it was over. Four warriors lay on the ground. Quickly reloading, I searched the forest for their ponies, finding a bay, a sorrel, and two paints in a small clearing.

I took the bay. The animal wore a hackamore.

We went through the dead men's plunder, taking what little we could put to use. Besides a few strips of dried jerky and a bag of pemmican, we found cartridges, knives, and two Winchesters. Their handguns were old and loose fitting.

Wind Whistle and I looked at each other, the same question racing through each of our heads. "Maybe more," he muttered, almost inaudible.

Grabbing a handful of mane, I swung onto the bay. "Then we best ride with a keen eye."

But it wasn't the keen eye that saved us. It was our keen hearing.

After dark, the Apache struck.

Chapter Twelve

Earlier, we had picked up Kiowa sign a few hundred feet north of the Apache ambush. I deferred the tracking to Wind Whistle while I kept an eye peeled on our backsides.

The trail led higher and higher as the afternoon grew shorter and shorter. From time to time whenever we approached a natural site for ambush, we pulled off the trail into the understory vegetation and scouted ahead on foot.

Just before dusk, the trail rounded a rocky bluff and disappeared down a narrow corridor into the oak and hickory forest. Wind Whistle reined up. He nodded to a grotto in the face of the bluff. "We camp here."

The sun was crimson red in the west. I wasn't anxious to pull off the trail, but there wasn't more than half an hour's light to work with, and the grotto was an ideal camp against attack.

"Fine with me."

We rode around a chest-high ridge of rock to enter the grotto, which arched twenty feet deep into the granite and quartz bluff. A cold spring bubbled from the ground.

Dismounting, Wind Whistle indicated a small heap of ashes. "Make small fire. I be back." Without explanation, he vanished into the forest.

Within moments, I had a small fire blazing. As if on signal, Wind Whistle returned with a dead rabbit, which he quickly skinned, gutted, cut into chunks, and roasted over the small fire.

We dispatched the rabbit and doused the fire. By now, darkness had filled the forest, but no thicker than the chorus of night sounds filling the air.

I lay on the saddle blanket with my Colt cocked. Behind me, the horses grazed on the lush grass around the small pool of water.

We remained silent, motionless, waiting for the inevitable.

Don't believe the stories about Indians not fighting at night. There might be some, but the Apache isn't one of them.

It was hours later when I heard the first sound, a light scraping, like the wind blowing the head of a weed against a rock. Except there was no wind. Slowly I rose to a squat.

The bay and paint behind us nickered and shuffled about.

The noise could have been a snake, a feeding rabbit, a stalking fox. But I knew it was none of them. I remained motionless, peering into the complete darkness, trying to pinpoint the Apache's position from the sounds.

Another faint scratching joined the first, then another. I figured three with a fourth tossed in for good measure. I squinted into the night. I could see nothing. How in the blazes could those Apache find their way without creating some commotion?

Without warning, a faint scrabble of tiny feet broke the silence, eliciting a gasp of breath from one of the stalking Indians about halfway to my left, less than five feet distant.

I swung my six-gun and fired.

The night lit up, for a brief moment illumining the startled face of an Apache brave. In that flicker of an eye, I saw two more Apache warriors at his side. I jumped to my feet and emptied my six-gun in the direction of the braves.

On the far side of the grotto, Wind Whistle was firing, but I had no time to pay him any attention. In the same motion, I holstered my handgun and drew the other.

I leaned back against rear wall of the grotto, straining to peer into the darkness, made even darker by the orange-white glare of the gunfire that had almost blinded me. All I could see was a fuzzy orange ball slowly diminishing in size.

In the next instant, there came a rush of padded feet and a solid weight struck me in the chest, driving me off my feet and onto the hard ground. My handgun flew into the darkness.

Legs straddled my belly. I jerked upright, ducking my head. At the same time, I felt the warrior swing his war club over my shoulder. With as much force as I could muster, I smashed the top of my head into his face, knocking him backward.

He swung the war club again even as he slammed on his back. I leaped at him, throwing up my arm to ward off the blow. I hit, jamming my shoulder into his neck.

Finally, I managed to grab the hand holding the war club. His breath was rancid. I grabbed my knife, and drove it into his side.

With a sharp jerk, I ripped across his belly. The warm stench of offal and blood assailed my nostrils. The warm liquid soaked through my denims.

A searing pain shot through my shoulder, and I realized he was biting me. Abruptly, he stiffened, then relaxed and went limp.

I rolled off him and lay without moving. All I could hear was harsh breathing from the far side of the grotto mixed with the nervous stampings of our ponies. I drew my feet under me. My left hand throbbed. I flexed it and almost screamed. I bit my lip and studied the shadows of the grotto, trying to pinpoint Wind Whistle. "You okay?" I whispered.

Wind Whistle replied softly. "Yes. We must be silent. There may be more."

I didn't think so, but there was no sense taking chances. My hand throbbed. I clamped it under my arm and settled back into a dark niche and awaited morning. A few minutes later, I felt liquid warmth soaking into my shirt beneath my injured hand.

Laying my six-gun in my lap, I felt my left hand. My little finger throbbed something fierce. I felt for it.

A cold chill raced through me. Hot blood spurted against my palm with each beat of my heart. My finger had been chopped off.

I removed my neckerchief and wrapped it around my hand, stemming the flow of blood. I clamped it back under my arm and leaned back, clenching my teeth against the sharp pain, peering into the darkness, wishing for the morning.

Finally false dawn grayed the sky. I made out the fuzzy outline of Wind Whistle. He looked at me. "Maybe no more."

I eyed the dead Indians lying about the camp. "I hope not. You have mescal?"

He cut his eyes to my hand clamped under my arm.

I held up the bandaged limb. "Lost a finger."

That satisfied him. With a grunt, he fished a button of mescal from his possibles bag and tossed it to me. I popped it in my mouth and chewed it well.

Within minutes the intensity of the pain began to subside.

In the meantime, Wind Whistle built a small fire and heated the blade of his knife. I unwrapped my hand and held it out to him, blood spurting anew.

He seized my hand with one of his tightly and in a

swift move pressed the blade to the nub. The air crackled with sizzling flesh and a tendril of burned smoke curled up.

I grimaced and cursed.

Wind Whistle sheathed his knife. He shook his head when I started to lower my hand. "Not yet."

From his possibles bag, he pulled out a small piece of cactus and pressed it against the nub. "Now put rag back on."

By the time I bandaged my finger once again, he had swung onto his pony and headed him down the trail after the Kiowa.

I climbed into the saddle and followed.

Mid-morning, a thunderstorm savage as a meat axe roared through, washing out the Kiowa trail and driving us into a cave. We chewed on some jerky and ate a handful of pemmican. Wind Whistle gave me another mescal button.

Impatiently, I stared at the rain. Not even Wind Whistle would be able to follow Standing Fox's trail now.

I muttered a curse and stared blankly at the pelting rain. The limbs of a sweetgum sagged almost to the ground. Rivulets of water were beginning to run down the mountainside.

The only satisfaction I could take was that the Kiowa were probably holed up too.

Wind Whistle squatted beside the fire as he laid a branch on it. "We go to *Aux Arc*. Standing Fox will come."

"How far?"

He held up a finger. "One sun. Not far."

The Kiowa camp was small, no more than a dozen or so teepees. Long racks fashioned by saplings held row after row of split trout drying in the sun. The size of the band answered a couple questions I had puzzled over. Kiowa country was back west, and I had wondered why they had moved into the Ozarks.

But now, I saw the tribe had not moved; only a few families who were scouting for better summer hunting.

The first warrior I met was Black Buffalo, Standing Fox's father. Quickly, Wind Whistle explained my mission as we stood outside the older warrior's teepee.

Black Buffalo looked at me with sad eyes. "It is no good for father to lose son. But, the boy is not mine to give. He belongs to Standing Fox. You will speak with Standing Fox." He looked at the gouge on my forehead. "He do that?"

I nodded. "Yep. Him or one of his friends."

Black Buffalo studied me a moment. "You will stay in our camp. You have nothing to fear."

"Thank you. But, if your son gives you the boy, couldn't you give the boy to me?"

With a brief shake of his head, he replied. "No. I would be insulting my son by giving away his gift to me."

I considered his answer. It made sense to me.

The camp was hospitable. Wind Whistle took me into his home, and for the next two days, they treated me well. The first day, five of the warriors took me to a small river for fish. Leading the way was a young brave with a bright smile and a ready laugh. Wind Whistle's nephew, the son of his second brother, Tall Horse.

I looked over my shoulder. A dozen Indian women tagged after us, carrying woven baskets. "They think we're going to catch that many fish?"

Wind Whistle grinned. "You see."

At the river, a stockade trap had been constructed. In the shape of a Y, it spanned from the riverbank to the middle of the river. At the base of the Y, openings led to three different boxes, each five feet square and filled with rolling, twisting trout churning the water.

I whistled in amazement as the women deftly seized the fish and deposited them in the woven baskets.

"Come," said Wind Whistle, following the other warriors a few feet up the riverbank to a roll of hand-tied netting. "We catch more."

The netting stretched sixty feet, from the middle of the river to the far bank.

For the next hour, the six of us held it in place, diverting fish into the trap.

We feasted and danced that evening. I dropped off to sleep dog-tired and with a stomach about to burst.

The Kiowa were fine people. I hoped Standing Fox wouldn't dispute my claim to Homer. I touched my fingers to the scabbed-over gouge in my forehead and studied the nub of my finger. Both wounds were healing.

Chapter Thirteen

If I had not been worried over Homer's welfare and concerned of Standing Fox's reaction when he saw me, those two days with the Kiowa would have been among the most pleasant I had passed in years.

I found them an honorable, honest, and happy people. I lay awake that last night thinking of the how idyllic the life must have been before the white man began pushing the Indians off their native lands.

The next morning, I was squatting at the breakfast fire in front of Wind Whistle's teepee when Standing Fox rode in. Beside him was Homer astride my dun. The other three Kiowa braves rode behind. Standing Fox jerked his pinto to a halt and glared malevolently at me.

Homer opened his mouth to yell at me, but I shook

my head quickly. I didn't want to put the Kiowa brave on the prod any more than my presence already had.

I remained as I was, casually chewing on baked trout and boiled plantain. My hand was still sore, but the pain had subsided considerably.

Standing Fox leaped from his pony with his fists clenched, staring at me. Abruptly, he turned and strode across the clearing to his father who had emerged from his teepee.

Throughout the camp, other Kiowas stepped outside their teepees to watch.

Standing Fox halted only inches from Black Buffalo. I couldn't understand their palaver, but the wild gesticulating and the occasional dark looks Standing Fox threw at me made it clear he wasn't about to invite me to a church box supper.

Wind Whistle spoke softly to me. "He will come to you next. Either to challenge or to return the boy."

"Which to you think it will be?"

"He will fight. Knives and warclubs."

I glanced at my bandaged hand. Knives and warclubs. That was all I needed. I drew a deep breath and started to rise to my feet.

Suddenly, their voices ceased. I looked up in time to see Black Buffalo send Standing Fox staggering backward with a sharp slap of his hand.

The young Kiowa warrior, his body trembling with rage, glared murderously at his father. Abruptly, he spun and leaped on his pony. He wheeled it about savagely and dug his heels into its flanks. With a wild cry, he drove the pinto down the trail from which he had emerged only minutes earlier.

His three comrades stared at each other, indecision scribbled across their faces. Hesitantly, they turned after him and disappeared into the forest, leaving Homer behind.

As soon as they were out of sight, Homer slid off the dun and raced to me. He hugged me about the waist. "I'm sure glad to see you, Mister Forrest. Real glad."

I laid my hand on his head. "You all right, boy?"

He looked up, nodding rapidly. "Yes, Sir. I am now."

Glancing at Wind Whistle, I whispered, "What happens now?"

"The boy is for any to claim. Standing Fox did not give him to his father."

"Then I claim him."

Moments later, an older woman, her deerskin dress greasy and dirty, rushed up and grabbed for Homer. Wind Whistle laid his hand on her arm and spoke quickly.

She glared up at me, then spit on the ground and stormed away.

"She wanted the boy. I told her you had claimed him."

I looked after the angry woman. She stopped at a small cluster of Kiowas and spoke rapidly, jabbing her finger at me angrily. The warriors glared at me.

"It is time for you to leave," Wind Whistle said under his breath.

There's a time to run, and there's a time to fight. I clearly saw this was the time to run.

I grabbed Homer and heaved him up on the back of the bay I had taken from the dead Apache. I paused, turned to Wind Whistle, and offered my hand. "Thanks."

He took my hand and nodded. "Go."

I swung up on my dun and took the west trail, avoiding the southern one down which Standing Fox and his braves had disappeared. Homer followed, bouncing up and down on the bay like a rubber ball.

Twenty minutes later, I reined up and switched ponies with Homer after shortening the stirrups on my saddle for him. Now we could make better time.

Standing Fox remained in the back of my mind. I didn't understand all that had taken place back in the Kiowa camp, but I knew enough to realize that any proud, young warrior who had been shamed in front of his own people and his prize taken from him would not forget the humiliation.

We rode until after dark and then camped cold. Jerky and water was our supper. Homer slept soundly. I dozed, awakening at every sound, each time expecting to see shadowy figures leaping on us.

The next morning, we rode out with false dawn. I had grown up on horseback and had grown accustomed to the rigors of travel, so I had to remind myself to pull up occasionally so Homer could take a rest.

But I never forgot Standing Fox. He was out there in the forest somewhere.

For some reason, I thought about Judith Brooks and Lena Hudson, the two young women who had torn each other's hair out over Cole Haywood. I wondered if they were still fighting.

Four days later, we reached Fort Gibson and the wagon train.

Homer's return was cause for an impromptu celebration, after which his mother threatened to blister his hide if he ever pulled another such fool stunt.

For the first time in days, I put myself around a solid meal and enjoyed a whole night's sleep without having to awaken to attacking Apache or Kiowa. The nub of my little finger was healing.

Before we left Fort Gibson, Virginia Lea Miller and the other three discontented ladies pulled out. "It just isn't worth it, Mister Forrest," said Virginia. "We just can't stand this kind of life."

I understood. "I spoke with the Major in charge here. You ladies will be able to hitch a ride back to Westport from here," I replied. "Good luck." In a way, I felt sorry for them. Sometimes you have to risk it all to acquire the best in life.

So, leaving four of our group behind to await the next stage, we forded the Arkansas and then the Canadian River, which we followed west. We were entering the Ouachita Mountains. While not as tall as the Ozarks, the area of the Ouachitas through which we had to travel was more rugged.

And then the rain began once again. Warily, I kept

an eye on the river. To my consternation, it began to rise.

I pushed the ladies harder.

After two days of driving rain and hard travel, Lay and I reined up along the side of the trail as the wagons splashed slowly past. Katherine Stanton came to us. "You're running the wheels off the wagons, Mister Forrest. May I ask why?" Water dripped from the sagging brim of her hat.

"The river's rising."

She glanced at the Canadian. "So the river's rising. We can pull farther back from the shore."

"There's the hitch. Two days downstream, the river runs through a gorge. When I came through, the river was down, and we brought the cattle through without any problem, but if the river rises much more, it'll flood the gorge. We'll be stuck for no telling how long unless we take the trail above the river."

She arched an eyebrow. "Well, then we take the trail."

"Not if I can help it," I replied.

Katherine frowned. "Why not?"

"Narrow and rough. A wrong step and . . . well, I'd just as soon not take a chance."

Neither she nor Lay spoke, but both knew what I was implying.

Nature goes her own way, and no jasper can figure her. It makes no sense that the good die young and the bad grow rich, but it happens.

That's the only answer I had for what happened when we reached the gorge.

The Canadian roared through it at twenty feet, a violent, churning cascade that had ripped giant trees from the ground and sent them tumbling downriver.

Our only luck was the rain had passed by mid-morning, and now the sun was breaking through the clouds. At least, that's what I thought.

The sheer granite walls of the gorge rose a hundred feet above the flood and bordered it for over a mile before descending back down to the river's bank.

"What do you think?" Lay nodded to the flooding river.

"A week. Maybe more. And that's with no more rain."

He muttered a curse. "Looks like we got no choice. Let's take a look at the trail above."

I grimaced. "I'd just as soon wait a week or so than risk the trail."

With a crooked grin, he replied, "It won't hurt to take a look. Besides, who knows when the rain will start up again."

Lay and I studied the narrow path leading to the trail a hundred feet above the river. Fractured prom-ontories of granite hung menacingly over the trail. I turned to Cole. "Hold everything here. Lay and me'll see what's ahead."

We urged our ponies up the steep slope to the trail. Lay whistled softly. "When you said narrow, you meant narrow. There's no more than three or four feet to spare."

I had ridden the rim when we brought the herd through weeks earlier. There had been a few small boulders dotting the trail. Nothing so large a couple strong backs couldn't roll aside.

The iron horseshoes on our ponies clattered against the granite as we ascended the trail. At the top, I winced as I thought of the oxen traversing the narrow trail. Only a mile, but a mile of sharp, slashing granite. We'd be mighty lucky to get the oxen across without any serious injuries.

The wall of an ox hoof is tough horn, but I had seen them split, which crippled the animal. I was more worried about the bulb, the back part of the animal's hoof that was composed of soft, rubbery horn. The jagged granite could slice the bulb into bloody shreds.

We rode the length of the trail. Other than a few small boulders, which we rolled aside, it was clear.

Lay studied the narrow road. "I think we can make it. Don't you?"

I had misgivings. "I could. And you could, but I don't know about the ladies." The trail was only a couple feet wider than the wagons.

He shrugged. "We're going to have some mighty short tempers if we sit around a week or so. And like I said, who's to say we won't get more rain."

He had a point. We only had a few feet to spare, but if the wagons remained close to the side of the gorge, we should make it without any problems.

Back at the wagons, I gathered the ladies. "First, we wrap the oxens' hooves against the sharp granite. We don't want to cripple none of the animals if we can help it."

The ladies nodded soberly, their faces reflecting their fear and worry.

I grinned. "We can make it, but you have to be mighty careful. Walk on the inside of the trail. Keep the wagons between you and the edge. Lay will lead the way. I'll fall in the middle. The boys will bring up the extra oxen after the wagons are over."

Bertha Lewis tugged her hat down on her head and nodded. A few ladies eyed the raging river fearfully. I couldn't help noticing Judith Brooks and Lena Hudson holding on to each other. Hard to believe they'd been trying to claw out each other's eyes just a few weeks earlier.

I signaled to Lay. He waved back and headed up the trail. Elijah followed in the chuck wagon with Homer. Katherine Stanton followed, leading her wagon, and one by one, the others followed, rattling and clattering as they banged over the fractured granite. The driver walked beside the off leader carrying her Moses' Stick. The other ladies of the wagon followed single file, taking care to stay close to the granite walls.

Overhead the sun beamed down on the wet granite. A soggy, uncomfortable heat enveloped us. Below, the rampaging river thundered and roared.

My dun stutter-stepped nervously, but I kept his head toward the inside of the trail. "Easy, boy, easy."

Behind, the wranglers finally came in sight. Maybe we would make it without trouble.

The frightened bawl of an ox erupted above the clatter of bouncing wheels and rattling wagons. A terrified scream sent chills through my blood. "Snake!" I looked forward in time to see a team of oxen humping their backs and kicking.

The team behind the terrified oxen balked, then tried to turn, but Bertha Lewis held them in check.

Before I could open my mouth, the first team lunged toward the rim. The leaders tried to stop, but the swing and wheelers kept bawling and pushing. On the far side of the team, a blond head bobbed, and a shrill voice screamed.

I tore my lariat from its leather and swung out a loop. Not wanting to frighten the animals any more than they were, I hoolihaned it over the wagon. Suddenly, the leaders dropped out of sight over the edge, jerking the blond head with them. My loop snapped around nothing but air.

In the next second, the entire team and wagon vanished over rim and hurtled into the churning river.

Judith Brooks ran screaming to the edge. "Lena! Lena!"

Behind me, Bertha Lewis crushed the rattlesnake with her Moses' Stick.

Chapter Fourteen

I leaped to the ground and rushed to the rim of the trail.

Below, the three yoke of oxen struggled frantically against the deadly current, which swept the wagon past the animals, dragging them backward. To one side, a blond head surfaced, then vanished.

"Lena!" Judith shrieked.

The other ladies stood frozen on the rim, staring at the cascading torrent below.

"Get back, ladies," I shouted, holding both hands over my head and waving them back. "Don't get too close."

Katherine Stanton elbowed through the crowd, her face white with horror. "Help her. You got to save Lena."

All their eyes turned on me.

"First, all of you get back to your wagons. We don't need anyone else to fall."

"Hurry up then," Katherine shouted. "Let's turn back and get her."

Several voices chimed in.

"We can't turn back," I shouted above the roar of the flood. "You've got to go ahead. I'll go back."

Lay rode up. "What happened?"

Quickly I explained, then added, "Lead them out of here. I'll pick up a couple wranglers at the rear, and we'll look for her." I tried to sound positive for the benefit of the ladies, but I knew it was hopeless. Still, there was always a chance.

Judith cried, "No. I won't go on. I've got to find Lena. Don't you understand?" I reached out to her, but she yanked her arm away. Her eyes rolled in panic.

I caught Katherine's eye and nodded to the hysterical woman. She hurried to Judith and slipped an arm around the screaming woman's shoulder. Nelly Jackson rushed to help. Together they managed to take Judith Brooks back to a wagon.

"Take them on, Lay," I said, leading my dun along the edge of the rim to the rear of the wagon train.

Reluctantly, the ladies continued, their horror-filled faces stained with tears.

I took the Allen brothers, Joe and Emmett, with me to search for Lena Hudson. A mile beyond the trail, we found half of the wagon caught in a tangle of trees. There was no sign of the oxen.

Joe Allen looked around at me. "Ain't no way she could have come out of that alive, boss."

With a brief nod, I agreed. "Maybe not, but we'll keep looking until dark."

We camped on the riverbank that evening. Emmett shot a young buck, and we roasted the backstrap. "I was ready for some fresh meat," he said. "And I reckon Elijah and the ladies will appreciate some too."

Normally, I would have relished fresh venison, but that night, everything I stuck in my mouth tasted like dirt.

Next morning, we continued our search. We found her at noon. She had washed ashore, and the animals had found her. Joe clenched his jaw. Emmett gagged and turned away.

I stared at her torn body, trying to push aside the turmoil of emotions flooding through my veins. "We best bury her here, boys. I wouldn't want the ladies to see her like this."

We wrapped her in my tarp and placed her in a shallow grave on which we piled boulders. "I reckon that'll keep the blasted animals away," Joe remarked, stepping back and eyeing the grave.

"Yep." Emmett agreed, his face flushed from the exertion of hauling rocks.

"Reckon so." I swung up on my dun and stared down at the lonely grave in the middle of a wilderness.

For the last thirty or so years, courageous settlers had pushed across the continent, searching for a new and better life. I once had an old trail guide tell me that there were at least ten graves to every mile of trail from St. Louis to the Pacific Ocean.

I stared at the grave and touched the tip of my finger to the brim of my sombrero. "So long, Lena," I whispered.

We reached the wagon train just after dark and broke the news. I expected a torrent of tears and crying, but to my surprise, only Judith shed tears, and then for only a moment.

I saw something in the eyes of the women, a strength that had not been present when the journey began, a somber realization of the rigors of their mission.

And that was exactly what it had become, a mission.

That night, while I squatted beside the chuck wagon and shoveled in the venison stew Elijah had whipped up with the young buck Emmett had killed, Katherine Stanton and Bertha Lewis, leading half-a-dozen or so ladies, approached. Their faces were somber with concern.

"Excuse me, Mister Forrest."

I looked up, then quickly rose to my feet. "Yes, Ma'am."

Katherine hesitated. From behind, Matilda Schaefer, her stub of an arm now healed, pushed forward. "Tell us about Lena, Howie. We'd like to know."

About Lena? My mind raced. I hemmed and hawed. "What do you mean?"

Katherine found her voice. "It might sound female

to you, Howie, but we'd like to know how she looked. She was a beautiful woman."

"Was she still beautiful?" Roly-poly Maude Perkins looked up at me hopefully.

I glanced down at Emmett Allen, who buried his head in his bowl of stew. I'd done enough in my life to assure that I had a permanent home with old Satan, so I figured another lie wouldn't bring about that much more fire and brimstone.

"Yes, ma'am. Just as beautiful."

Emmett glanced up, then looked back down.

"She looked like she was sleeping. Of course, her hair was all wet, but for the most part, she looked like she was sleeping."

My words must have satisfied them. The concern on their faces softened and tiny smiles played across their lips.

"That's good," said Katherine. Despite the dim light of the campfire, I saw a blush color her cheeks as she continued. "You might think it foolish women's non-sense, Howie, but even when a woman is in her grave, she'd like to know she is still pretty."

I'd never thought about that sort of thing. I just figured when a body was dead, he was dead. I'm not sure I understood exactly what she was saying, but I had the feeling the ladies were paying me a compli-ment of some sort by revealing what seemed to be mighty private feelings.

"Yes, ma'am." I nodded. "You can rest easy. She was just that."

After they departed, Emmett looked up at me, an

eyebrow arched. I growled at him, "Open your mouth, and I'll turn you into a steer."

He grinned. "You done good."

We were able to move out the next morning. I'd been concerned about the jagged granite slicing up the animals' feet, but other than minor scratches, they all made it over the trail without injury.

After leaving the Canadian River, we hit the Texas Road for our last leg to the Red River. At the Red, we'd take the Butterfield Route, which would take us beyond Jacksboro and Fort Griffin.

Maybe Mother Nature figured she dealt us enough bad hands. Maybe she decided now was our time for some good cards because the next couple weeks were uneventful.

We made camp on the north bank of the Red River.

"Why don't we cross before night?" Maude Perkins stared across the half-mile of sandy bed. "It's all sand. Only that small stream out in the middle." Two or three assenting voices sounded behind her.

"All sand and quicksand," I replied, waving my hand as a pointer. "I have to look it over first. Find a route."

"Quicksand?"

I scooted around in my saddle and looked at the ladies standing behind me. "Yep. Quicksand." They looked up at me, and I continued. "The river is full of it. If it catches you, escape is just about impossible. It'll suck you under."

They drew a collective breath and stared back at the broad riverbed.

Lay pulled up beside me. "Did you lose any cattle when you crossed?"

"Thirty-two head. Only lost eighteen more the rest of the drive. But at this river, we lost thirty-two."

Early next morning, Lay and I went out on the Red on foot, carrying an armload of stakes and a Moses' Stick to use as a probe.

"What's that for?" He indicated the stick.

"You can spot quicksand by the watery sheen on the surface. But, sometimes the quicksand is a foot or so beneath the surface. One or two wagons might make it over. Maybe all of them, but I wouldn't want to take a chance. A solid surface can give way mighty sudden. This way we can poke around for any hidden pits."

The young cowpoke shivered and looked down at his feet.

I laughed. "Don't worry. The ground won't drop out from under your feet. You'll have time—maybe," I added, grinning at his discomfort.

While the others watched from the north shore, we carefully picked out a narrow path across the half mile–wide bed. The stream in the middle of the bed was only inches deep and fifty feet wide. The water was clear as a freshly washed lantern globe.

"Why do they call this the Red River?" Lay asked.

"Up river, it cuts through red sandstone. At flood time, the water is dark red from bank to bank."

An hour later, we returned to the waiting wagons. I climbed in my saddle. "Ready, ladies?"

Carrying her Moses' Stick, Katherine Stanton stepped forward and laid her hand on the ribs of the off leader. "Take us across."

Several voices from behind chimed in.

I studied them a moment. The women had changed. It wasn't the clothes, although some wore men's denims. Others had packed away their fluffy slips and skirts, content with a lightweight shift. Rugged weeks of travel had trimmed and hardened their muscles. Their bright eyes looked up at me from tanned faces filled with confidence and assurance. I had to admit, I didn't figure this many would reach the Red. I admired them for what they had so far accomplished, yet we were still a long piece from Palo Pinto.

"Stay between the wagons, ladies. Don't wander beyond the stakes that mark the edge of the path. Keep moving. You feel the sand give, don't stop. In fifteen minutes, you'll be on the other side."

I nodded to Lay. "Move 'em out."

He wheeled about and rode slowly on to the Red.

Cole Haywood rode in the middle of the wagons.

At the rear, the wranglers had strung out the oxen and ponies in single file. The brothers, Joe and Emmett, led the oxen while Ed and Albert trailed the ponies.

I brought up the rear, my fingers crossed. I felt comfortable with our trail on either side of the stream. That fifty foot–wide expanse of water had me worried. The flow of water constantly moved the sand, one moment providing a solid surface, the next, a mix of water and sand that would suck an hombre beneath the surface in seconds.

Trouble started when the lead wagon hit the stream.

I heard a scream. Strange as it might seem, I immediately knew it was Katherine Stanton.

Suddenly, the wagons jerked to a halt.

I raced to the front, waving at Lay to continue. "Go around," I shouted at the wagons. "Keep moving. Don't stop. You'll sink."

Lay whipped a loop over the near leader of the second wagon and got them moving, skirting the first wagon whose front right wheel had sunk to the hub.

The wheeler oxen had bogged. Frantically, they struggled to free themselves, but the yokes hooked to the tongue held them in firm restraint.

Katherine was tugging on the leaders, trying to urge them forward. By now, the rear wheels had sunk to the axle.

I leaped from the saddle and yanked the tongue ring from the lead yoke, then unhitched the chain traces to free the yoked animals from the other two yokes. At the same time, Cole Haywood knocked the yokes from the oxen, freeing the pair from each other.

Once freed, five of the six oxen bolted across the river. The sixth was bogged to the hips. The white sand clung to his red curly coat. Time after time, he lunged, frantically trying to escape the ever-tightening grip of the quicksand.

Cole and me threw our loops on the bawling animal, but we couldn't budge him. We drove our ponies, stretching the ropes so tightly that water vibrated from the hemp. The ropes cut into the ox's flesh, choking him.

I reined my dun back, dropping the tension on the rope. "That's it. We can't do any more."

By now, water had seeped into the wagon bed. It was just a matter of time.

As the last wagon passed, I sent Katherine with it. "You can't do anything here."

She protested, but she did as I said.

The wranglers drove the other animals past. They shied, spooked by the frightened bawling of the sinking oxen.

"Keep 'em moving, boys," I shouted, staring helplessly at the ox, its wide eyes rolling in fear and desperation.

Cole grunted after the last of the remuda had passed. "Well, Boss. You want me to do it?"

"Nope. Reckon it's my place. You go ahead."

I waited until Cole had caught up with the wagons. I pulled my Colt. I don't know if the animal sensed his fate or not for he renewed his struggle, but the quicksand had sucked his hips under. He held his head high, eyes wide, bawling pitifully. Reminded me of an old mama cow who had lost her offspring.

Raising the Colt, I aimed at the middle of the animal's forehead.

Chapter Fifteen

The day was hot and still. We made another four miles before we set up camp. The river crossing had drained us, but at least we were now in Texas, a week or so from Lost Creek and couple to Jacksboro, about four from Palo Pinto.

We had begun our journey two months earlier with eight wagons counting Elijah's chuck wagon. We were down to six. We started with twenty-eight ladies and were down to twenty-three. Not bad, I told myself that night as I propped myself on my saddle under the wagon and sipped six-shooter coffee. Not bad at all.

Just before dark, a line of thunderstorms moved through, soaking us good, but helping replenish our water supply.

* * *

A hand shook me awake around midnight, and a hushed voice said. "Boss. Wake up, wake up. Trouble."

My eyes popped open at the word, "trouble." I looked up into the shadowy face of Joe Allen. "What's up?"

"Cole's gone. Him and that Judith Brooks sneaked out of camp."

I sat up and reached for my boots. "Blast! How long ago?"

"Don't know for sure, but that ain't the worst of it."

With my foot poised for the boot, I looked at Joe. "What else?"

"That Stanton woman went after them."

I jerked around and banged my head into the axle. I grimaced and cursed. I squinted through the pain. "She what? Why?" Angrily, I jerked my boot on. "Why in the blazes did she do an idiot thing like that?"

"Beats me. That's what Bertha Lewis told me."

I stomped through the camp to Bertha's wagon. I spotted her squatting by the campfire, pouring a cup of coffee. The large woman rose as I approached. "What the Sam Hill is going on?"

She arched an eyebrow. "Young kids, hot blood. That's how it goes."

"I told him to leave her alone."

She gave me a crooked grin. "And you figured that would take care of it?" She shook her head. "You might be smart with cows, but you don't know nothing about people, Trailboss."

She was right. My hackles were up for the wrong reason. "What about Katherine? Why'd she take off?"

Bertha sipped her coffee. "She figured she could get them to come back. She and Judith had become good friends. According to what she said, Cole had been after Judith to run off with him for the last few weeks. I guess the temptation got too much for her."

All I could do was shake my head. "Where'd they go? Any idea?" I glanced to my left, toward Fort Worth, a hundred miles or so to the south.

"They rode out to the east. At least, that was the direction Katherine took."

"How long's she been gone?"

"Couple hours."

I stiffened. "A couple hours? Why didn't you say something sooner? We could have gotten them back by now."

"I promised her I'd wait. Give her time to get them back."

All I could do was stare in disbelief. Slowly, I shook my head. "Well, Mrs. Lewis. All I can say is that you were wrong. You shouldn't have let her go. At the least, you could have come to me, and I would've stopped her." I shook my head. "Women!"

I rode out to the herd. Young Emmett admitted helping Katherine Stanton saddle her pony. "It was the sorrel she'd been riding, Boss. She said it was okay with you."

The bright stars cast his worried face in a bluish relief. "At that time of night? Blast, Emmett. Where's your brains?"

"I'm sorry, Boss. But she was mighty convincing. I told her I needed to ask you, but she said you'd rip off my hide if I woke you up, seeing as you'd taken sick." He hesitated. "You feeling better now?"

"What?" I shook my head, thinking I'd missed something.

"You know. You was sick. You feeling better now?"

All I could do was shake my head. Poor Emmett. I reckoned he was one of those unfortunate few who believes everything someone tells them.

"Emmett, listen to me. I was never sick. She told you that so you wouldn't wake me. Understand?"

He studied me a moment. The wheels turned slowly. "Oh," he finally said.

For the second time in a matter of weeks, I had to leave the wagon train. This time I packed some dried jerky, coffee, and a small bag of cornmeal. I might be gone one day or one month.

I pointed Lay and the wagon train southwest, using Joe and Emmett as point scouts. "Keep an eye for Kiowa and Comanche. Put two guards out at night."

Following Katherine's sign in the rain-packed sand, I headed east, toward Sherman, Texas. The countryside was cut by draws draining water northward to the Red River. Mid-morning, I rode into one draw where I discovered a passel of sign in the damp sandy bed. Three ponies, and only hours earlier.

Back in the crook of a bend were the ashes of a recent fire. The wind sweeping down the draw had scattered some of the ashes, which meant it was last night's, after the rain.

The trail led south. Two sets of tracks were older than the third. Not much, maybe two, three hours. The edges of the tracks were beginning to crumble.

An hour later, I reined up near a small pool of fresh water in the shade of a overhanging bank. I nodded as I studied the sign. I had been right. There were three sets, two almost filled with water seeping from the pool. The third set was about three-quarters full.

Katherine was about an hour, maybe a tad less, behind Cole and Judith. I urged the dun into an easy gallop. I took a couple sips of water and bit off a chunk of jerky. With luck, I should spot them anytime.

Without warning, the hair on the back of my neck bristled. I reined up and dropped my hand to the butt of my Colt. I saw nothing. An empty draw. White clouds in a pale blue sky above the rim of the draw.

With a click of my tongue, I pushed the dun up a narrow watershed, riding out of the draw so I could take in the surrounding country.

As far as the eye could see, rolling hills covered with short grass and sage stretched to the horizon. To the west, a dust devil swirled across the prairie. A quarter of a mile ahead, the draw cut back east.

And then a faint sound reached my ear. I cocked my head, straining to pick up the sound again.

A faint popping drifted from across the prairie.

Gunfire!

I slapped the reins against the dun's rump. He leaped forward, slid down the embankment and raced across the draw to the far side. In one leap, he scrambled up the bank and headed west.

The gunfire grew louder.

At the crest of the first sand hill, I pulled up and peered across the short grass and sage prairie. The sporadic gunfire came from the south. I dug my heels into my pony's flanks and sent him flying across the prairie toward the next sand hill. The sage and cactus blurred as we swept past, his long legs gobbling up the prairie.

At the top of the next sand hill, I jerked my dun to a stop. He sat down on his hind legs as he struggled to bring himself to a halt.

Down in a basin a half-mile distant, Katherine Stanton lay in a buffalo wallow, using her dead pony for protection against four painted Kiowas. Coolly, she fired her Winchester, holding the screaming warriors at bay.

My heart leaped into my throat when I spotted two riderless Indian ponies. My first thought was that they were slipping up on her under the cover of the sagebrush.

And then I spotted two sprawled figures in the sand. They wouldn't be sneaking up on anyone.

I yanked my own Winchester from the boot and slammed my heels into my pony's flanks and raced down the hill, standing in the stirrups and pumping one shot after another in the direction of the startled Kiowas.

They reined up, surprised.

Abruptly, a third somersaulted off the rump of his

pony as the report of Katherine's Winchester echoed over the thunder of hooves.

With a shout, the remaining Kiowa spun and raced to safety.

Katherine leaped to her feet and emptied her Winchester after them. I pulled up and quickly dismounted, my heart thudding against my chest. "Are you alright?"

She glared at me defiantly for a moment, then dropped her gaze. "Yes. I'm fine . . ." She paused. "But I lost my horse."

"You sure you're alright?"

She looked up at me quizzically. "Yes. I told you I was," she added with a touch of irritation in her tone.

Relieved, I exploded. "What in the Sam Hill did you think you were doing, running off in the middle of the night? And don't say you could take care of yourself, Missy, because you were right smack dab in the middle of a mighty sizeable mud hole of trouble."

For several moments, she glared up at me, her eyes icy, her jaw set. I didn't care if she was madder than two cats with their tails tied together. I glared back.

Her eyes softened. She dropped her gaze. "I'm sorry, Howie. I didn't think. I just wanted to try to talk some sense into Judith."

I wanted to stay mad, but I couldn't. "At least you're okay." I glanced around. "We'd better reload and light a shuck out of here. Those braves might be part of a larger band."

After climbing in the saddle, I swung her up behind

me. She wrapped one arm around my waist and clutched the Winchester in her free hand.

"How come you ended up out here? Their tracks continued south." I turned my pony to the north, hoping to skirt the Kiowa who had disappeared over the western horizon.

"I heard shots. When I came to see what made them, those six Indians jumped me."

Ahead, a dead Kiowa lay on the ground.

I started around him. Katherine gasped. "Howie!"

"What?" I reined up.

"That Indian. The bracelet."

"What about it?" The bracelet was made up of a half-dozen or so intertwined silver wires.

I felt her body shudder against my back. Her voice was tight with fear. "It's—it's Judith's. And look. He's wearing her locket too."

Praying she was wrong, I quickly dismounted and retrieved both items. I opened the locket and sudden weight hit me in the middle of my chest. On one side of the locket was a picture of Judith Brooks; on the other was a small child.

Wordlessly, I handed it to Katherine. Tears filled her eyes. She sobbed, "That was her little girl. She died when she was four."

Climbing back in the saddle, I studied the countryside around us. There was a slim chance Cole and Judith were still alive. As soon as I got Katherine back to the safety of the wagon train, I would try to find them.

I had planned on riding due south, circling the Kiowa and then cutting west to intersect the train, but now time was a factor. I had to take us southwest, roughly paralleling the flight taken by the Kiowa.

"Keep your eyes open. If the Kiowa are out there, we'd best see them before they spot us." I felt her nod.

In a thin, choked voice, she replied, "I'll watch."

Ten minutes later, we spotted the buzzards.

Chapter Sixteen

Not even the sweltering heat stirred a breath of wind across the sun-baked prairie. Overhead, the sky was a washed-out blue, a white bowl stretched from horizon to horizon.

Katherine's fingers dug into my shoulders. The creaking of the saddle, the scratching of the sand against the hooves, and her short, gasping breath were the only sounds breaking the scorching air that filled the lungs like blasts from a furnace.

She stifled a scream when a cloud of buzzards swirled out of a shallow wash and into the sky with angry and startled cries.

I reined up and studied the prairie around us. The Apache could hide in plain sight, a skill shared by other tribes. Fortunately, the Kiowa did not possess that talent. They were horsemen, a bareback cavalry unrivaled by any tribe or any army.

Still, a jasper had to be mighty careful.

We eased closer. "Stay here," I said, sliding out of the saddle and heading for the wash. "Watch the hills around us."

I stood on the edge of the wash and grimaced as I stared down at Judith and Cole. They had been stripped of clothing and jewels, but not mutilated, not by the Kiowa. The buzzards did a good enough job on that.

From the death wounds on the two, I instantly recognized that Cole had done that which had been necessary. Seeing that capture was inevitable, he shot Judith and turned the gun on himself. I shook my head. What a waste! What a blasted waste!

I buried them together in the wash, next to the bank, while Katherine watched for the Kiowa from the crest of a nearby sand hill.

Our eyes met when I started to climb back in the saddle. Each knew the other's thoughts. Each knew just how close Katherine had come to suffering a similar fate. I said nothing. The pitiful little grave of Judith and Cole shouted a louder warning than I could ever hope to speak.

We rode in silence, but in that silence, I sensed we had forged a special connection. I couldn't explain it. I couldn't even say for sure it existed, but the earlier feelings between us had changed.

We camped cold that night and next morning, caught up with the train just as it reached Clear Creek.

As soon as I rode in, I knew something was wrong. Faces were grim, and every woman carried her Winchester.

"Comancheros, I'm guessing," said Lay, gesturing to the horizon. "Looked like some Mexicans and a few Injuns. But, they kept their distance. We pulled the remuda in closer. The ladies kept their Winchesters ready." He grinned and nodded to Matilda Schaefer, the woman who lost an arm just after the trip began. She grinned back at him when he said, "I think them old boys out there are going to be some kind of surprised if they're thickheaded enough to ride in here on these ladies. Why, there'll be enough lead coming out of here to sink the Delta Queen riverboat."

After fording the creek, we continued southwest.

There were a few misty eyes when Katherine told the ladies about Cole and Judith, but no outbreak of tears and wailing. For a moment, that puzzled me. They were women. They were supposed to break down and cry. But these didn't.

I was beginning to understand that old Colonel Egerton was a heap brighter than I thought. He understood the ladies a lot more than I had, than I still did.

Sort of like a herd of buffalo. The strong keep going and survive. The weak fall by the side of the trail. That was the only explanation that made sense.

I'd seen evidence of that back at Fort Gibson when Virginia Lea Miller and the other ladies pulled out.

We had begun with twenty-eight and were down to twenty-two, with another three weeks ahead—probably three of the most rugged.

Texas weather comes in two seasons, summer and winter.

We were halfway through the month of September, that period most Texans consider the middle of summer. Heat rose in undulating waves, distorting the distant sand hills. The short grass prairie was dying from lack of rain. We lost Abraham and Gideon, two of Elijah's mules and a few of the spare mounts because of poor graze and scant water. The oxen just kept plodding along, maintaining a slow two-mile-per-hour pace. Durable creatures, they could feed on next to nothing and drink less than anything and keep on pulling.

The Comancheros Lay had mentioned kept out of sight, but from time to time, we found sign of a large party whose route paralleled our own.

For three days, we rode with our weapons cocked, ready to circle the wagons and dig in. For three days, the Comancheros remained beyond our sight, but ominous clouds of white dust billowing above the distant horizon told us they were still there.

We set out four guards at night.

The second night, Katherine came to my campfire. I rose. We hadn't said more than half-a-dozen words since our return, but as soon as she entered the glow of my campfire, that funny connection I'd experienced the other day returned.

She looked at me almost shyly. I gestured to the fire, and she sat. Joe Emmett nodded to her courteously. She cut her eyes to the darkness. "What about them out there? What do you think they'll do?"

I studied her a moment. There was no fear in her eyes. Two months earlier, I would have expected to see some, but now, her lack of fear came as no surprise. "Hard to say. They know we're short on men and long on women. Could be they're biding their time, hoping we'll get careless so they can come in."

She looked at me levelly. A strip of white skin just below her hairline marked the set of her hat. Below the ribbon of white, her skin wore a richly tanned glow that enhanced the determination of her set jaw. "They do, and they'll get their eyes opened."

I grinned at her. "Reckon so. In the meantime, however, we'll keep on keeping on with our eyes open."

Katherine fell silent. After a few moments, she started to rise. I spoke up quickly, for some strange reason not wanting her to leave even though she had been a burr under my saddle since the trip began. "How are the ladies all doing?"

She looked at me for a moment, her eyes opening in surprise, which she quickly covered by glancing at Joe, who had laid back on his saddle and flopped his sombrero over his face. She sat back down. "Oh, they're all doing fine. Just fine. Ready for the trip to end." She wore a faint smile that was mighty becoming. Her eyes seemed to sparkle.

"Well, won't be long." I hesitated, uncertain if I

should say what was on my mind. I shrugged. Why not? "Truth is, Miss Stanton, I . . ."

"Please. Call me Katherine, Howie. We've been together out here on the trail long enough to be on a first-name basis, don't you think?"

I nodded. "Reckon you're right—Katherine."

The campfire danced off her sparkling eyes. "Now what were you going to say?"

"Oh, only that you ladies have done real good. I didn't think you could make it, but you've proved me wrong. There's a heap of grit and determination in you ladies."

Her smile widened. "Why, thank you, Howie. That pleases me a great deal to hear that."

I leaned back, a feeling of warm satisfaction flooding over me. "You want some coffee?"

"No. I'd like to just sit here and look at the stars."

"There's a heap of them," I replied, staring up at the bowl of glittering diamonds over our heads, after which I immediately cursed myself for making such an inane observation. Sure there were a heap of them. Any idiot could see that.

But my obvious declaration didn't seem to bother her. She cleared her throat. "You have a spread of your own somewhere?"

"No, Ma'am." I shook my head. "I figure on finding a small place north of Fort Worth. "That's back east of here about a four- or five-day ride. Wide open spaces. An hombre can stand on a hill and see for miles."

She hugged herself and smiled. "Sounds wonderful."

"What about you?" I paused and cleared my throat. "If you don't mind me saying so, you're a right handsome woman. What are you coming out here for? Seems to me that..." My words stuck in my throat. I hemmed and hawed, fearful I might have offended or embarrassed her.

Katherine laughed. "Seems to you that I should have been able to find a man back East?"

I shifted about nervously, cursing myself for even bringing up the subject.

The merriment in her eyes faded. She continued in a hushed voice. "I had a family. A son and a husband." Her voice dropped lower and her eyes focused on the fire. "Phillip, my husband, died in the war. At Chancellorsville. My boy, Martin, died of cholera. I was a school teacher, and I could have stayed in Crystal Bluff, but it held too many memories. I wanted a fresh start."

She grew silent, staring at the fire. Finally, she drew a deep breath, threw back her shoulders, and replacing one personality with another, gave me a bright grin. "And this offer from Colonel Egerton seemed just like what I was looking for. He was a good man. I wish he could have been around at the end."

Grateful she changed the subject, I agreed. "He would have been mighty proud."

"Well, Howie, how much farther do we have?"

"Like I said, not long. A couple creeks to Jacksboro and Fort Belknap. After that, a week and we'll have you ladies in Palo Pinto where you ladies can get all hitched up good and proper."

Her tiny smile froze, then faded. Her eyes slid away from mine. "Yes. I guess you're right. Not long." She pushed herself to her feet. "Not long at all," she added in a flat voice as she turned back into the night.

I stared after her tongue-tied. What the blazes had I said that caused her to change moods like a sunfishing bronc swaps ends? I looked to Joe, but he was sawing logs.

That night, I couldn't get to sleep. Usually, ten seconds after my head hits the saddle, I'm snoring away, but that night, I lay with my hands behind my head, fingers laced, staring at the starry sky and trying to sort the mixed feelings running through my brain, what little I had of a brain.

I wasn't completely dumb about women. After replaying our brief conversation a dozen times over, I decided that the only thing I could have said to upset her was about her getting hitched. But, it didn't make sense to me that that would upset her. After all, that's why she made the trip.

Chapter Seventeen

I must have dozed, for when I jerked awake, the campfire was burning low. Rolling out of my soogan, I tossed another log on the fire and shook Joe awake. The two of us had the next shift with the herd.

From time to time in my ramblings, I'd hear proper folk talk about fine art. They'd throw around foreign-sounding names and gush over how some jasper managed to paint such a fine picture. I don't know about that, but I can tell you that the Texas prairie at night is as fine a work of art as the Good Lord could ever make.

From horizon to horizon, the black sky is encrusted with glittering stars that seem to force an hombre to wonder just what lies out beyond them. The distant cry of a lonely coyote climaxes the beauty of the night, sort of like the last page in a book.

Not that the night has no dangers. They are there, but knowledgeable cowpokes know how to avoid them. Listen carefully, and you can hear a snake gliding over the sand, or the absolute silence of lurking Indians.

The herd of oxen and ponies stood contentedly, half-dozing, then awakening to graze a few minutes before dozing once again. Time passed slowly. As I circled the animals, I heard a faint noise off to my left. Peering into the darkness, I spied a darker shadow standing motionless.

I froze, straining to make out the object. Taking my time, I eased the loop from the hammer of my trigger. The figure moved, and a familiar voice whispered, "I come as friend."

For a moment, I failed to place the voice, then I remembered. Wind Whistle! What was he doing here? "Come ahead."

Like a ghost, he appeared at my side astride a paint war pony. "Standing Fox come for boy."

Quickly, I scanned the dark countryside, seeing nothing. "When?"

He pointed to the west. "He joins with the Comancheros. After they kill the men, they will take the women and boy to Mexico. Much *dinero*."

I hated to admit the truth, but I was skeptical although Wind Whistle had never given me any reason to be so. I guess the fact he was a Kiowa was enough to color my feelings. "Why do you tell me this?"

He stared at me. The bluish light cast by the stars filled his eyes with shadows, but cast the set to his jaw in sharp relief. "Shame has come upon my house. Never had one in my family turned Comanchero. I would see Standing Fox dead before I will return to my wickiup and look my people in the eye. We are a proud people. I know the time is soon that White Eyes will come in great numbers, but even then, I will still have pride."

I believed him. "How long?"

"With the next wind. They plan to burn the grass." He made a sweeping gesture to the prairie.

Grimacing, I looked out over the rolling hills. A prairie fire. With oxen, we weren't about to outrun anything, especially a racing prairie fire. "How many warriors and Comancheros?"

Wind Whistle shrugged. "Many."

That could have meant ten or twenty—or thirty.

He added. "More than the fingers on your hand two times."

My blood ran cold. In a low voice I called out, "Joe. Over here."

Moments later, the young wrangler rode up. "What's up, Boss?" He failed to notice Wind Whistle.

"Go fetch Emmett and Ed. Tighten the herd. We're moving out as soon as we can."

He stiffened when he saw Wind Whistle. "Who's that with you? Hey, that's—"

"Hold it, Joe," I barked. "This here's Wind Whistle. He's a friend." Hastily, I explained our problem. "I'm going in to wake the camp. We're yoking up and lighting a shuck out of here."

On the way back to camp, Wind Whistle said, "You have many women, few men. What do you plan?"

In the east, false dawn lightened the sky.

"You'll see." I rode by the wagons. "Roll out, ladies. We're heading out. Yoke up."

A chorus of muffled protests rolled through the camp, but when they spied Wind Whistle at my side, they knew something was amiss. Quickly, they rolled up their blankets, loaded the wagons, yoked the oxen, and grabbed their Winchesters.

Wind Whistle looked at me in surprise when he spotted the rifles. I nodded. "They can use them. Fifteen shot. Twenty-two women and six men, seven counting you. Them Comancheros have themselves a big surprise if they try to run over us."

"But, what of the fire? Rifles cannot stop the fire."

I peered into the dim grayness of the early morning. "No, but if I can find the right spot, we might be able to handle the fire."

Before we moved out, I laid the cards on the table for the ladies. "We can whip this, but I can't have any of you ladies breaking down on me. No one."

I left Lay in charge. "Move 'em south as fast as you can. Don't let anybody lag behind."

Wind Whistle and I rode out. "Scout to the southwest. Look for a riverbed."

A faint smile played over his lips, and his dark eyes glittered with understanding.

"You find something, fire two shots in the air, count

three, then fire two more and then hightail it back to the train."

He nodded. "I do."

I pushed my pony hard, keeping in mind what I covered in twenty minutes would take the oxen an hour. And we didn't have that many hours to waste. With early morning came a gentle breeze, but as the sun rose and heated the countryside, the winds picked up.

I rode in vain. As far as the eye could see, thick, dry grass and sagebrush made brittle by the heat covered the rolling prairie like a blanket. A prairie fire would roar through here in seconds, consuming all that stood in its way.

Thoughts, confusing thoughts, tumbled through my head. Could Wind Whistle be playing me for a dunce? Maybe he thought by getting me away from the train that the Comancheros might have an easier time. But if that was what he was up to, why didn't he shoot me when he rode up in the dark this morning?

Half an hour later, two shots, a pause, then two more reports interrupted the argument I was having with myself.

For a moment, I hesitated, once again reminding myself that Wind Whistle was Kiowa. What if—? Abruptly, I reined my pony around. "No," I muttered under my breath. "This is no betrayal." I dug my heels in my dun's flanks. I was committed.

After several minutes, the train came into sight, and far to the west, a ribbon of dust billowed into the blue sky. Despite the battle that lay ahead, a sense of relief washed over me. I had been right about Wind Whistle.

He pointed to the southwest. "Three, maybe four miles. Dry riverbed. Maybe wide from here to last wagon." The distance he indicated was less than two hundred feet. That was cutting it close, but given the alternative, we had no choice. I gestured hard to the southwest. "Take us there."

He looked at me, his sun-darkened face revealing no emotion. Without even a nod, he led out. Elijah fell in behind. I rode along the line. "Push 'em hard, ladies. We got an hour, maybe two to work with."

And they pushed the oxen hard. Katherine carried the Moses' Stick for her wagon, continually prodding the usually somnolent oxen. Behind her, Maude Perkins, Bertha Lewis, and Nelly Jackson, along with her son, Homer, urged the oxen at a faster pace. Bringing up the rear, Matilda Schaefer, the Moses' Stick cupped in the crook of her stump, prodded her yoke of cattle.

The other ladies strode purposefully beside their wagons.

No one spoke. I saw the fear in their eyes, as I imagine they could see in mine, but not a solitary soul whined, not a solitary eye shed tears, not a solitary hand shook.

Jaws set and eyes filled with determination, they marched through the heat and dust.

I sent Emmett to the west, to watch for the fire. "Let us know when you see it."

* * *

The wind intensified.

Heads of grass began waving.

The leaves of the sagebrush rattled in the strengthening breeze.

The first faint signs of the prairie fire reached us minutes later, the terrifying, acrid smell of burning grass mixed with the stringent odor of sage. And then tendrils of smoke drifted past, light and tenuous at first, but growing thicker by the minute.

I looked around for Emmett. He was watching for the fire. Where in the blazes was he?

Wide-eyed, the oxen bellowed and bawled. They tried to run, but the ladies held them with their lead ropes.

"Keep hold of them," I shouted.

The smoke grew thicker. I whipped off my neckerchief and soaked it with water and tied it over my nose. The ladies did the same. We blinked against the sting of the smoke.

In the distance, I spotted some shallow bluffs. The riverbed! And beyond the bluffs was a row of sandhills. I squinted into the smoke for Wind Whistle, but he had vanished.

"Hold on to them, ladies."

"Howie. Howie!" Emmett slid his pony to a halt. He wheeled about and pointed to the west. "It's coming. Over the hills yonder. I never seen anything like it. It's twenty feet high."

By now, the ladies were running, desperately trying to hold the frightened oxen. Without warning, the remuda stampeded, racing through the wagons in panic while the wranglers tried to hold them in check.

"Forget the stock," I shouted. "Throw your loops over the leaders. Hold them back." Each of us snugged our rope around the leader of a wagon and reined back, slowing the frightened oxen.

All except for Elijah. Before we could put a loop around one of the mules, the frightened creatures grabbed the bit in their teeth and broke across the prairie. The chuck wagon bounced and rocked, and with each jerk and movement, utensils and boxes flew from the wagon.

Lay screamed above the bellowing of the oxen and the rattle of the wagons. "Jump, Elijah! Jump!"

Without warning, the chuck wagon struck a shallow wash and bounced into the air where it literally fell apart, unfolded—as if every bolt and nut had come loose at the same time.

The bed flew through the air. Axles and wheels whipped in opposite directions. The canvas top and oaken hoops popped straight up. And Elijah went spinning head over heels, his arms and legs flailing.

The mules disappeared into the smoke.

Lay threw off his rope and raced for Elijah.

The last I saw before the smoke swallowed the two, the young cowpoke leaped to the ground and dropped to his knees by the still form of the old man.

Suddenly, we were at the riverbed.

"This way," I yelled, leading the first wagon across the riverbed to the base of the bluff.

Leaping from the saddle, I grabbed the lead yoke

on Katherine's wagon and yanked the restraining pin, freeing the oxen from the wagon tongue. "Drop the traces," I yelled.

Katherine unhitched the trace chains, and the three yoke of oxen lumbered away into the smoke. Quickly, we unhitched the other teams, leaving the five wagons in a square in which the ladies took refuge.

"The oxen!" Katherine coughed and gasped. "They're running away."

"We'll worry about that later. I—" My words stuck in my throat when I saw the raging fire sweep over the sandhills and race across the prairie toward us. I dropped to my knees. "Stay low." Because of the bluffs and hills behind us, the heavy smoke swirled upward.

I blinked at the smoke stinging my eyes and slapped at the embers burning my skin.

Suddenly, scores of rabbits darted across the river-bed followed by antelope, wolves, coyotes, and a myriad of other animals.

I crossed my fingers, hoping the narrow strip of sand would halt the raging inferno. The intense heat radiated across the dry riverbed. I felt like someone had tossed me in an oven and slammed the door.

Burning sparks swirled about us. A canvas top burst into flames. "Rip them all off," I yelled as Joe tore down the burning top.

Moments later, the roar of the inferno abruptly ceased. I peered through the smoke. Where a ten-foot wall of fire had raged seconds before, now only a few small patches of dying flames remained.

The riverbed had stopped the firestorm.

I turned to Joe. "You stay here with the ladies. You other old boys come with me."

Old Ed Dowling frowned. "Whereabouts?"

"Up there." I indicated the fifteen-foot crest of the bluff overlooking us. "We'll carry a couple of the ladies' trunks and build us a barricade against any attack from behind."

Emmett jumped up in one wagon and yanked on a trunk. "Oooff. Blazes. This thing is heavy."

"Dump it out. Quick. If the Comancheros are going to hit, it'll be in the next few minutes. Ladies, now's the time to show just how good you learned to use those Winchesters."

Seeing the doubt in some of their faces, I hesitated. "Take your time. Just remember before you squeeze the trigger that if those Comancheros take you, they plan on selling you to the highest-paying brothel in Mexico."

Shock, then anger replaced the doubt in their faces. Katherine looked at me levelly. "Don't worry about us, Howie." She patted the butt of her Winchester. "We know what these are for!"

A chorus of agreement and shaking of heads echoed her words.

With Ed and me carrying one trunk, and Emmett and Al the other, we built a hasty rampart on the bluff, and then settled down to wait.

The smoke was quickly thinning.

Keeping his eyes forward, Ed Dowling squirted a

stream of tobacco on the ground. "You reckon Lay bought a patch of ground?"

"Last I saw, he went after Elijah."

Emmett spoke up. "Sure hope he's—hey, here they come," he yelled.

Throwing up a cloud of black soot and sand, a band of Indians and Comancheros swept over the crest of a sand hill a hundred yards south of the riverbed. When they spotted the pitifully small cluster of wagons, they let out a bloodthirsty howl and began firing.

"Steady, ladies," I called out, sprawling on my belly and searching the charging renegades for Standing Fox. I wanted him first.

Chapter Eighteen

Below, the ladies rested their rifles on the wagon beds, steadying their aim.

I shouted down, "Not yet. Wait until I fire. We want 'em in close. And when you start shooting, don't stop."

The charging renegades hit the riverbed. At that distance, even a greenhorn stood a good chance of at least hitting a horse, and these ladies had proven they were far removed from being greenhorns.

Quickly, I scanned the skirmish line bearing down on us. No sight of Standing Fox. There was no more time to waste. "Now!"

As one, twenty-seven Winchesters fired, sending a lead barrage smashing into the charging Comancheros. Two or three were knocked from their saddles. Half a dozen horses stumbled. Their front legs collapsed, sending them tumbling head over heels, smashing their riders underneath them. The firing continued unabated. The startled Comancheros reined up, which proved to be another mistake.

The Winchester .66s were not heavy rifles like the old Henrys and Sharps, but their firepower more than made up the difference. Another seven or eight Mexicans and Indians dropped. Riderless horses raced across the prairie.

I peered through the gunsmoke, searching the milling Comancheros for Standing Fox. No luck.

Horses reared and pawed at the sky. Desperate outlaws clung to the backs of wildly spinning animals. Frantically, the Comancheros tried to fight back. I heard slugs ripping into wood. Once or twice, the sand near my shoulder exploded.

Firing methodically, we continued raking the decimated band of renegades.

A guttural shout cut through the confusing melee of gunfire and screams. I spotted a fat Comanchero wearing a red sash and riding a white horse gesturing frantically to the renegades. Suddenly, they turned tail and raced away. We threw several wild shots after the fleeing outlaws.

Below, over a dozen Comancheros and Indians lay sprawled in the sand.

The four of us checked the fallen Comancheros. They were all dead except one, a young Kiowa brave. He had a slug in his right shoulder and his left leg had been shattered below the knee. For a moment, I thought he looked familiar, but I dismissed the thought. All Indians looked alike.

Ed Dowling spat out a stream of tobacco and cocked his Winchester. "Blasted savage don't deserve to live."

I knocked the muzzle away just as he fired. He glared at me. "There's been enough killing," I said, meeting his stare.

Emmett spoke up. "Well then, Boss," Emmett said with a wry tone. "You got a problem then. You just going to let him lay here and die? Or what?"

By now, the ladies had gathered around, hanging on to every word we said.

I looked at the young brave grimacing in pain. He couldn't have been much over fourteen or so. Only a couple years older than Homer. I didn't answer Emmett. Instead, I looked over the ladies. "Anyone here hurt?"

Maude Perkins held up her battered sombrero. "Got me a hole in this, Boss. That's all," she said to a chorus of nervous laughter.

"I got a burn on my arm," said Bertha Lewis, showing a bloody furrow on her shoulder.

"Well, ladies. I need a volunteer. Got a shot-up Kiowa boy here. One of them that tried to take you to Mexico. I'll patch him up, but I need a wagon to haul him on to Jacksboro where we can turn him over to the authorities."

Without hesitation, Katherine stepped forward. She gestured to Emmett and Al. "Put the boy in the back of my wagon. I'll tend his wounds," she added, looked up at me.

I smiled at her. "Thanks."

While she tended the boy, I sent the wranglers out after the stock, some of which could be seen grazing in the distance. And then I spotted two objects even farther beyond the feeding cattle.

The lingering smoke covered the prairie with a haze in which distant objects seemed to blend into one another. I squinted into the smoke and made out two horses, the first with a rider apparently leading the second pony. I studied the rider a moment. As he drew closer, beginning to emerge from the smoky haze, I recognized Lay by the way he sat his saddle. A smile leaped to my lips, but immediately vanished when I saw what appeared to be a body draped over the saddle on the second horse.

A sense of foreboding enveloped me. I shook my head, praying the limp form was not Elijah, but I couldn't shake the sinking feeling in my belly.

I hoped against hope.

And then, my hopes crashed.

I saw the old black head with the ring of gray hair bobbing with each step taken by the horse. Behind me, I heard a soft gasp.

Lay reined up. "Broke his neck when the wagon crashed." He hesitated, fighting back the tears filling his eyes and threatening to spill down his freckled cheeks. "I . . . I just couldn't leave the old man out there all by himself."

For several moments, I stared at the back of Elijah's

head, thinking of all we had lost on the trip. I looked around at the women standing motionless, staring at the dead man. I had never been given much to praying, but right then I prayed that this journey worked out like the Colonel had planned. If not, there would be a heap of good people wasted for nothing.

I laid my hand on Lay's knee. "You did right, Son. We'll give him a proper burial here."

We buried Elijah on the top of the bluff overlooking the riverbed after which we put the dead Comancheros in a common grave, not as much as out of respect for the dead as to avoid the stench and circling buzzards.

The next two days, we stayed busy rounding up stock and patching gear. We lost half-a-dozen ponies, Elijah's mules, and almost half the oxen, forcing us to go to a two-yoke team instead of a three.

Finally, the evening of the second day, we were ready to move out. "Sunup," I announced. "We'll move out at sunup."

Around the campfire, the talk turned to the wounded Kiowa boy. Ed Dowling spat a stream of tobacco juice into the fire. While it sizzled, he growled. "I still think you made a mistake by not blowing that blasted heathen's head off, Howie."

I shrugged. "Maybe so. And if he'd made another try at us, I would have. But . . . well, think I'll check on the ladies before I turn in. You and me got the second shift tonight."

The fires were burning low as I stopped in at each wagon and visited with the ladies for a few moments.

They were in good spirits and ready to move out. Given the distance we'd traveled from Westport, Palo Pinto was just over the horizon.

Katherine was changing the Kiowa boy's dressings. "He'll have a limp from now on," she said, indicating the splinted leg. "But at least he'll be able to walk." She smiled at the boy. For a moment, the sullen frown on his dark face faded, replaced with a faint smile of gratitude.

"Reckon the next couple days to Jacksboro will be hard on him, bouncing along in the wagon."

She nodded. "We'll cushion the bed best we can."

I studied her for several moments, amazed at the compassion she displayed toward the Kiowa youth.

She knit her brows when she realized I was staring at her. "What?"

"Huh? Oh, nothing."

"No, it wasn't just nothing. What were you thinking about?"

I figured I wasn't going to get away without telling her something, so I opted for the truth. "It was just that I didn't expect that you, a white woman or any white woman, would take such good care of an Indian."

Even in the dim light cast by the dying fire, I saw the blush creep into her cheeks. "He . . . he's not just an Indian. He's a boy." Her face grew somber. "Mine died, but I'd like to think that had he lived and been injured, some other mother, maybe even an Indian mother, would have tended him. I . . . ah . . ." Her voice faded away. And the firelight glittered on the tears welling in her eyes.

My own throat choked up. I laid my hand on her shoulder. "Best get some rest. We got a big day tomorrow."

Lost in thought on the way back to my fire, I failed to see a shadow glide from around the rear of my wagon. When I looked up, Standing Fox was glaring at me, his Winchester aimed at my belly. His dark eyes glittered. "I say I come back for boy. Now I come."

Ed started to rise, but the Kiowa brave pointed the muzzle at him. "You move, old man, I kill you," he said, keeping his eyes on me. "Now, the boy. Bring me the boy."

I shook my head. "No." I nodded to the darkness. "Leave. You will be killed if you try to take Homer. Leave now while you can."

His lips twisted in a sneer. "Old man. Get the boy. Or I kill this man."

"Don't move, Ed."

Raw anger twisted Standing Fox's face. I leaped aside and grabbed for my six-gun, thumbing back the hammer as I rolled on the ground. A single shot broke the silence of the night. I clenched my teeth against the impact that never came. I swung my revolver around and froze.

Standing Fox stood rigid, his rifle at his side, his eyes wide with surprise, staring down at the dark blood spurting from the hole in his chest. He pressed his left hand to his chest in an effort to stop the spurting, and then pulled his hand back and stared at it in shock. He tried to twist around to see behind him, but his muscles refused to obey the commands his brain struggled to send.

With a groan, he dropped to his knees, then sprawled forward onto the sandy bed.

Wind Whistle stepped from the darkness into the firelight, smoke still coming from the muzzle of his old Hawkins.

Around the fire with the entire camp looking on, the old Kiowa explained how he had been pursuing Standing Fox the last two days since the prairie fire. He had lost him back west and decided to return to the wagon train. "I surprise when I find him here. He the son of my brother, Black Buffalo. But he kill so much that it is sickness." He tapped his head. "He not right. Best Standing Fox live with his family in sky."

I told him of our battle, and of the Kiowa youth.

Wind Whistle looked at me in anger. "The Comanchero deserve to die. This one of which you speak. Though he Kiowa, he too should die. Why he live?"

"Just a kid. And he was hurt." I rose. "Come. He is in that wagon," I said, indicating Katherine's.

For the first time in my life, I saw Indian stoicism crack. A smile leaped to his lips when he saw the boy. "Small Elk!"

The Kiowa youth's eyes grew wide. "Wind Whistle."

A murmur of surprise raced through the camp.

Wind Whistle turned to me. "This Small Elk. He the son of my brother, Tall Horse."

That's when I recognized the boy. He was the one who led the fishing party those few days I enjoyed the hospitality of the Kiowa camp.

"Who is he?" Katherine looked up at me.

I explained. "He is Wind Whistle's nephew."

The ladies whispered to each other.

But now, I found myself in a quandary. Take the boy to the law in Jacksboro, or break the law and turn him over to his uncle who had saved my life?

There was nothing to think about.

Looking over the ladies, I cleared my throat. "By law, the boy should be turned over to the army for trial and sentencing. But, I'm not going to do that. I'm giving the boy back to the uncle to replace the nephew he killed to save my life. If any of you want to report me to the authorities when we reach Jacksboro, I won't try to stop you."

No one said a word.

"Can the boy travel, Katherine?"

She smiled at me. "Yes."

"Joe. Bring the boy a pony." I turned to Wind Whistle and offered my hand. "I reckon his uncle wants to head back home."

As the two Kiowa disappeared into the night, Katherine came to stand by my side. "You know, Howie. If you hadn't given the boy back to his uncle, we would have."

I chuckled. "Why doesn't that surprise me, huh?"
She laughed.

A week later, we crossed Lost Creek and headed for Jacksboro.

Chapter Nineteen

Jacksboro was a small community of less than a dozen adobe and stockade buildings, several in ruins, around a dusty square. Comanche and Apache raids had devastated the town during the war, and reconstruction was slow because of lack of hard currency.

After a two-day layover, we turned south, crossing Keechi Creek a few miles out and Carroll Creek just before sundown. The rolling hills were becoming steeper and the soil grew thinner, dotted with rocks and boulders of white limestone. We were leaving the treeless plains and heading into the oak and cedar forest of Central Texas.

We kept a close eye for any marauding Comanche or Apache. Word back in Jacksboro was that some Indians had been spotted skulking about.

"How good do you know this part of the country,

Lay?" We were astride our ponies on a rocky bluff overlooking a broad valley thick with hickory and oak.

The freckle-faced young man shrugged. "I've ridden through here a few times."

"Enough to keep us out of trouble with these wagons?"

"Reckon so, but we best scout ahead just to make sure we don't run into a dead end."

Two days later we reached the Clear Fork of the Brazos. Well, actually, we didn't reach it. From atop a ledge of granite, we stared over a slope thick with stunted oak and cedar at the river three hundred feet below.

I looked to the west. The river made a gradual curve to the north. Back east, the river cut sharply to the south. We were on the rim of a gorge that stretched from horizon to horizon. The ladies gathered at the rim and stared at the water far below.

"Well, reckon there's only one thing to do. Ladies, we camp here. Lay, you and Joe head east. Me and Emmett will go west. Look for a crossing."

Joe grunted. "How far do we go?"

"Back here in twenty-four hours unless you find one sooner." I studied the tableland around us. "Let's move back from the rim, back in the oak and cedar. Maybe our fires won't stand out too much. Ed, you and Al keep a close watch while we're gone."

"I can help."

I looked around at the high-pitched voice. Homer

stared up at me. "Reckon you can, boy. Al, keep Homer here busy."

Al grinned. "Yeah, Boss."

We rode out, and found nothing except steep slopes covered with oak and cedar.

"Same way back east," Joe said after we returned the next day. "Five or six miles downriver, the west bank opens onto a prairie, but on this side, the escarpment goes on as far as we could see."

Lay nodded his agreement.

I studied the river below. "Even if we made it down to the river, we'd still have the other side to climb."

A small voice spoke up. "No, you wouldn't." Homer stepped forward.

"What are you talking about, boy?" Lay frowned.

Homer glanced at his mother sheepishly and nodded to the river. "I went down there this morning. It isn't even knee deep. We could drive the wagons down the riverbed."

Nelly Jackson gasped. "Homer!"

I looked at Lay who arched an eyebrow. "How far did you go, Homer?"

He pointed to the first bend. "I was afraid to go any farther." He glanced sidelong at his mother. "Mama told me to stay away from the river."

Joe spoke up. "It might get deeper downriver, Howie."

"Float the wagons," Homer said. "Tie logs from wheel to wheel. I seen men doing that back at Westport Landing on the river."

Lay looked at me. "That might work."

I studied the river. "Come on, Lay. Let's you and me take a look at the river."

We returned an hour later. "Homer was right. The sand is hard-packed enough to support the wagons." I studied the faces looking up at me. "What about it, ladies? That means we have to cut a road down this slope to back the wagons down."

Bertha Lewis removed her floppy hat and dragged a large forearm across her forehead. "Well, Howie. I don't see we got a choice. Me, for one, I ain't about to turn back. There ain't no trees going to stand in my way."

A chorus of approval greeted her words.

So we set to work.

I put one team of ladies to splicing enough rope for two thick strands over three hundred feet in length. "Why so long?" Katherine asked.

"We tie the ropes around the tongue, and the other ends to the oxen. Stretch 'em tight, and then just back the oxen toward the edge. The wagon'll ease down to the river."

It was simple plan. I hoped it worked.

Two days we labored. One team felled the timber, another sawed it into manageable lengths, and still another hauled it aside, clearing a trail to the river.

Finally, we reached the river.

I lowered my axe and looked back up over the trail cleared to the top of the gorge. No sense in wasting time. We climbed to the top.

"All right, first wagon. Let's start it down. Joe, you and Emmett go down with it. It might need some muscle over some stumps or boulders."

"We can help," said Maude Perkins. "We got muscle. Come on, girls."

Katherine and Bertha backed the oxen.

To my surprise, everything went as we planned.

By evening, we had all the wagons at the river. We kept the stock on the rim until morning.

Next morning, we hitched up and headed down-river.

We traveled easy on the hard-packed sand. Once or twice, we hit deeper water, but never so deep as to float the wagons. By dusk, we reached the broad plains and rolled out of the river.

Lay grinned. "I know where we are now." He pointed up a long valley to a dark ridge of rugged hills to the south. "There's a pass cutting through. Palo Pinto is on the other side."

Word spread quickly. An undercurrent of laughter and nervous chatter filled the air above the rattle of chains and squeaking of wood. The months of discomfort were forgotten.

I scooted around in my saddle and looked over the wagon train. A sense of pride swept over me. We were coming to the end of a long journey that had thrown every scrap of trouble at us it could muster, and we made it through. I was right proud of those ladies.

We camped on the riverbank that night.

* * *

As usual, before sunup, we moved out, angling across the broad valley for the pass through the hills. From time to time, I spotted sign indicating recent camps, but I chalked it up to drifters.

And as usual, I was wrong.

Chapter Twenty

We reached the pass at dusk. The pass was a narrow trail ascending the rugged hills to the crest, about a thousand feet above our heads. Sheer walls of gray rock loomed over it. I wasn't anxious to tackle that kind of journey at night, so we camped at the base of the pass that night despite everyone's impatience to complete the journey.

"Smart move," Lay said as we squatted around the campfire. "This side is tricky. About halfway up, the west wall falls away, and the trail hangs on the eastern wall. There's a couple twists or turns there that could drop a jasper five hundred feet. Once we reach the top, we're okay. The road is straight as a pool cue, about half-mile down to the prairie. Palo Pinto's a couple miles from there."

We moved out with the sun next morning. Joe and

I led the way up the trail, both staring up at the fifty-foot walls towering over us. In a low voice, he muttered, "I'm glad we got no enemies, Howie. I ain't never seen no better place for an ambush."

I chuckled. "Me neither, Joe. Me neither."

Just as Lay said, halfway up the trail, the west wall fell away, ripped from the hills by earthquakes in the far distant past. "Take care, ladies," I called out, dismounting and leading my dun.

Once or twice, the steel rim of a wheel came mighty close to sliding off the trail. Each time, I held my breath, then released it with a sigh of relief as the wagon continued.

I looked ahead to the crest. I was relieved to see the pass once again had a west wall. I preferred the closed-in feeling between the two walls instead of a five hundred–foot drop off on one side.

At noon the last wagon reached the crest. We pulled in tight. "Take a break, ladies. Give the animals a chance to breathe."

And that's when a barrage of gunfire exploded in the pass.

I gaped in stunned disbelief as Lay and Joe spun out of their saddles. I was standing beside the dun, my hand on the saddle horn, when something stung my hand. I jerked it back and saw the horn was ripped open.

In the next second, I grabbed my Winchester and shouted, "Under the wagons."

The firing continued. Horses squealed and raced for safety. Slugs ricocheted off the rocky ground at our feet. I threw myself under the nearest wagon and rolled around so I could get a shot at whoever in the blazes had come after us.

Suddenly, a head appeared over the edge of the rim above, and I snapped off a shot. The bushwhacker screamed, rose to his feet, and tumbled head over heels to the trail. As soon as I saw his dress, I knew who was after us.

Comancheros. Probably those we'd run off back at the dry riverbed.

I studied the frightened faces of the ladies hunkering under the wagon with me. Katherine, Bertha, and Nelly Jackson were under the next wagon. Under the third one, I spotted Emmett with some of the ladies. Homer and the rest of the ladies crouched under the fourth one. Al and Ed huddled under the last wagon.

We were in a state of mass confusion.

Lay and Joe lay sprawled on the ground. Beyond them, two ladies lay motionless.

When Emmett spotted Joe, he cried out and jumped from beneath the wagon. A half-dozen slugs splattering at his feet drove him back under.

Slugs ripped into the wagons.

"It's the Comancheros, Emmett. They got us in a hole."

"That's what they think," shouted Katherine, throwing her Winchester to her shoulder and firing wildly at the rim. Bertha and half a dozen other ladies joined in.

"Save your bullets," I yelled. "Pick a spot on the

rim and wait until you see someone. That's the only way."

Behind me, a scream broke through the gunfire. Al leaped from under the wagon and collapsed. His body jerked three more times as three more slugs slammed into him.

Ed started cursing. He jumped from under the wagon and began firing at the rim.

"Get back under there, Ed," I yelled. "Get—"

An invisible club knocked him back against the wagon, then bounced him forward. Two more slugs made sure.

And then the firing ceased.

I looked at Joe and Lay. Were they dead? What about the two women beyond? We couldn't leave them there. "Ladies, we got to get our wounded in and take care of them. When Emmett and me take off, keep the old boys up there busy."

The ladies did just exactly what they had to. Emmett and I got the ladies first, then Joe and Lay. We were lucky they were still alive. We tended their wounds best we could under the circumstances.

Several minutes passed.

"What are they up to?" Katherine called from under her wagon.

"Just waiting."

"What are we going to do? We can't stay here."

I had no idea. My mind raced, looking for a solution. I considered sending Emmett into Palo Pinto. If we could get some more ammunition from the wagons, we could put up a sustained barrage of gunfire to keep the Comancheros down until he got away.

But when I looked, there were no horses. They'd all spooked. So much for that idea. But, we still needed the ammunition. "Emmett. When I give the word, jump up in the wagon and toss a box of cartridges out." He nodded. "Okay, ladies. Give us some help. Now."

A barrage of gunfire erupted from the wagons. Emmett and me jumped up in the wagons and fumbled for the boxes of cartridges. Not one shot was fired at us.

We managed to pass enough cartridges along for half a dozen reloads for each Winchester. I grinned.

A single shot broke the silence, followed by the startled grunt of an ox and then the clatter of chains against the rocky ground. I looked around just as a horrified voice cried out. "They're shooting the animals."

Even as she screamed, another shot rang out and another.

"All right, ladies. When I give you the word, keep them owlhoots up there busy again. Emmett, we got to go back out. Turn the animals loose. You hear? Just unhitch the ring and trace chains and leave 'em in yoke. They can make their way out of here."

He swallowed hard. His face was pale, but he nodded. "I did it before. I can do it again, Boss."

"And don't waste no time. We got fifteen shots to get it done."

"Don't wait for me."

"Okay, ladies. Now."

Emmett and me jumped out, with Katherine and Bertha right behind us. Winchesters roared. I didn't take time to look up, but I knew every last one of those jaspers up there was keeping his greasy head down.

I figured somewhere between thirty and forty-five seconds is how long it would take the ladies to empty the fifteen-shot magazine in the Winchester.

Bertha and Emmett worked toward the back, and Katherine and I toward the front. We unhitched the first set of chains without a snag. A stubborn bolt and nut slowed Katherine on the second. I had finished the third by the time she got the nut from the bolt.

Suddenly, the firing ceased. We dove for the wagons.

We watched in silence as the oxen half-trotted, half-stumbled down the slope toward Palo Pinto. Lay had been right. This part of the pass was straight as a pool cue.

Beyond the pass, the land opened up. As long as they had us in here, we were like ducks frozen in a pond. And come night, they'd probably start grabbing.

And then I had an idea.

Emmett arched a skeptical eyebrow as I explained my plan. Bertha shook her head, and Katherine rolled her eyes. "Let me get this straight. We hook two wagons together, load everyone in them, and then just roll down the hill. How are you going to steer the thing?"

"The wagon tongue. Fold it back and I'll use it to steer with."

"What if we run into the wall?"

"Are we going to be any worse off than we are now? If we're still in this pass tonight, Emmett and me won't see the sun in the morning. And you ladies, those of you still alive, will be bound for Mexico."

Bertha cleared her throat. "You ever done anything like this, Howie?"

I arched an eyebrow. "When I was a youngster, I rode a sled down a snow-covered hill."

She stared at me thoughtfully. "That don't seem like too much of a qualification."

"Reckon not." I shrugged. "Anyone else?"

No one spoke. "Alright. Ladies, help me push this wagon forward a few feet." On our hands and knees beneath the wagon, we shoved it forward until we had to place a rock under a wheel to keep it from rolling down the steep slope.

"Now, keep them Comancheros busy. Fire slow. Whenever a head pops over, run it back. Emmett, we'll run the tongue of the second wagon over the rear axle of this lead wagon and chain it to the bolster. Okay, let's get the tongue."

The ladies kept the Comancheros pinned down, and Emmett and I managed to hook up the two wagons.

We were ready.

At each moment, I expected the bushwhackers to figure out what we had in mind, but their tequila-soaked brains failed to fathom our intent. That and the fact that the ladies were turning into mighty fair sharp-shooters that kept the Comancheros ducking.

Under protection of the ladies' gunfire, we hurriedly loaded the wounded and piled the ladies in the two wagons. From where they sat in the wagons, they fired at the rim.

I threw the wagon tongue back, then drew a deep breath. I looked up at Katherine. "I sure as blazes hope this works."

She smiled warmly at me. "It will."

A startled shout from above told me the Comancheros had figured out what we were up to. I kicked the rock from under the wagon wheel, gave the wagons a push to get them rolling, then jumped aboard, grabbing the wagon tongue and struggling to keep the front wheels straight.

Slugs slammed into the wagon as it picked up speed.

We rattled and banged over the rocky surface. Screams mixed with gunfire echoed in my ears, but the wagons continued to pick up momentum, hurtling down the slope.

I shouted at Katherine. "Jump up here on the seat and put your foot on the brake. We get going too fast, these wagons might bounce to pieces."

We were being bounced around like dice in a cup. Katherine could barely stand, but she managed to clamber up on the seat and place her foot on the brake.

"Not yet," I shouted. The gray walls flashed past, fuzzy blurs.

"Now," I shouted above the clamor of screams and banging steel and booming gunfire.

She hit the brake. The back wheel caught, and the wagon veered to the left. I cut the wheels to the right, away from the granite wall.

We struck, and skidded along the fractured granite walls in a showering of sparks and the rending shriek of tortured steel. Shards of broken granite cut at my face.

"Keep the brake on," I yelled above the clamor of screams and gunfire and shouts, all melding into an unintelligible cacophony of sounds.

Something burned my side. I ignored it, struggling to hold the vibrating tongue steady. Behind me, Bertha shouted, "We're losing them. We're losing them."

Slugs continued slamming into the wagon, ricocheting off the towering walls. It didn't seem to me we were losing them.

Ahead loomed the end of the pass, and beyond open spaces where at least we had a chance to fight them off instead of playing fish in a barrel.

Suddenly, a dozen Comancheros appeared in the middle of the pass, some of whom were trying to roll a boulder into our path. Katherine screamed, "There. Ahead."

"Get them, ladies," Bertha shouted, turning her Winchester on the owlhoots in front of us. A dozen Winchesters opened up behind me. I cringed as the slugs hummed past on either side.

Four Comancheros dropped, and the others scattered.

Without warning, a heavy weight struck the back of my leg, almost knocking me out of the wagon. I fell against the wagon tongue, and the wagon swerved. I managed to yank it back as the pain from my leg struck me.

The firing continued all about me.

I yelled over my shoulder, "Shoot them, not me."

Warm blood ran down my leg. And then we shot past the Comancheros. They threw a few wild shots at us as we swept by. I heard a few grunts and shouts from the wagons, but I had too much on my hands to pay any attention.

We hit the prairie, and the wagons began slowing.

Before I knew what happened, a powerful force knocked the tongue from my hand and slammed it to the ground. For a moment, the tip of the tongue skidded along the ground before jamming into the side of a shallow wash and coming to an abrupt halt, lifting the front wheels of the lead wagon off the ground.

The tongue snapped, dropping the wagon back to the rocky prairie, smashing the front wheels. Bodies flew from the wagons. The momentum of the second wagon shoved us another forty feet before grinding to a halt.

I hit the ground hard. Stars exploded in my head, but I struggled to my feet. My right leg wouldn't work. I cursed it and beat it with the muzzle of my handgun. I know that did no good, but I managed to hobble back to the wagon, shouting for the others to take shelter behind the two busted hulks of wood and wheels.

The band of Comancheros charged down off the

ramparts above the pass. "Get ready, ladies. We got to do it once again." I glanced around for Katherine. She was nowhere to be seen, and then I spotted her, sitting on the ground and shaking her head some fifty yards distant.

"Katherine! Run! Run!"

She looked around and shook her head once again, trying to get rid of the cobwebs in her head.

Bertha shouted, "Run, Katherine! Hurry!"

She looked around and saw the approaching Comancheros. Struggling to her feet, she measured the distance to us, and the distance to a small copse of oak. She broke for the patch of scrub oak.

At the same time, the fat Comanchero with the red sash and riding a white horse spotted her. He jerked his horse around and dug his spurs in its flanks, racing after the fleeing woman. I recognized him as the leader of the scurrilous band.

I leaped over the wagons and hobbled toward Katherine. She spotted me, and ran toward me. We met in the open, and I shoved her behind me.

The Mexican spurred his horse, planning on running me down. I palmed my Colt and placed two shots in front of the horse, causing the animal to abruptly swerve, sending the Comanchero spinning from the saddle.

He hit the ground hard. To my surprise, he bounced to his feet and grabbed for his sidearm. I squeezed off a shot.

I thought I was fast, but he was the best I ever saw. Before I knew what was happening, a slug caught me in the shoulder, knocking me back against Katherine. I was lucky, for my first shot spun him around, spoiling his aim.

He jabbed the muzzle of his handgun at me, but I was already firing my last three shots, all of which would have fit inside a playing card right over his heart. He dropped before he could get off another shot.

I looked around quickly at the other Comancheros, expecting them to be bearing down on me, but instead, they had stopped, all staring at their fallen leader.

A guttural voice from one of the remaining Comancheros echoed across the prairie, and as one, they turned their ponies and headed southwest.

At that moment, a gunshot sounded from the direction of Palo Pinto.

Katherine helped me back to the wagons, where we all watched as a small band of cowpokes rode toward us.

"Remember, Howie," said Bertha, glaring down at me. "We ain't going in 'til we have a chance to look proper for our men. And it's up to you to see they understand that."

I looked back over our trail to the wagons still perched on the crest of the pass and the trail of clothing and goods spread along the trail in between. I grimaced against the pain in my leg. "Reckon we can camp right here tonight, ladies. You just make yourselves comfortable, and I'll give them old boys instructions on what to do."

Maude Perkins stepped forward, her eyes cast

down. "I didn't mean to shoot you, Howie. I just wanted to get one of those Comancheros. Is it bad?"

I laid my hand on my bloody leg. "Nothing busted. It'll be fine."

With a beaming smile, she rushed forward, stood on tiptoe, and kissed me on the cheek. "I'm glad," she said, backing away and dropping her gaze back to the ground.

I looked over my ladies once again. As one, they grinned at me, tanned faces smudged with road grime and powder, hair windblown, dresses sun-bleached and tattered.

They were the most beautiful women I'd ever seen in my life.

I hobbled out to meet the approaching riders. Katherine fell in beside me, giving me her shoulder to lean on. I frowned. "I thought you didn't want your man to see you like that? For all you know, he might be one of them yonder."

She looped her arm around mine. "No, he isn't one of them. Besides, he's already seen me like this."

For a moment, I didn't understand what she said, but when she smiled up at me, I knew. A silly grin plastered itself across my face, and I figured instead of the three thousand dollars the Colonel offered, I'd take those four sections of land along the river. Looked like I would have use of it now.

Conwell, Kent   NOV   2001
A wagon train for brides

GAYLORD M